YEEHAW JUNCTION

Kayli Scholz

MOONSTRUCK

BOOKS

PRAISE FOR YEEHAW JUNCTION

Yeehaw Junction is one of the bleakest slices of nihilistic rural noir you'll ever read. It's a stellar piece of work about squalid lives lived not on the margins of society but instead in a more homeless place somewhere beyond, a place where the forgotten and the shunned do whatever it takes to survive and the most ruthless predators are always on the prowl. Read it. It'll scar your soul.

—Bryan Smith, author of *Depraved*

Yeehaw Junction is sweaty. It's gross. It's weird. An injection of Spanish Moss directly into your nightmares. It's a horrific unraveling of events, like watching cars piling up on an exit ramp as a baby stroller rolls away, but you can't stop looking.

—William Sterling, actor, director,
author of *Fame by Misadventure*

"It's just the way it is sometimes; you're not wanted at the diner downstairs from the titty bar." *Yeehaw Junction* feels like Fernanda Melchor novelizing *Gummo*. Kayli Scholz's style of sleazy trailer park narration will leave you feeling implicated in the sickliest of ways ... This is the fastest I've read anything in a while.

—Ira Rat, author of *Participation Trophy*
and publisher at Filthy Loot

ALSO BY KAYLI SCHOLZ

Saint Grit

Black Rain Season

Moonstruck Books
Portland, Oregon
moonstruck-books.com

This is a work of fiction. All characters and events portrayed in this novel are fictitious and are products of the author's imagination. Any resemblance to actual events, or locales or persons, living or dead are entirely coincidental.

ISBN (paperback) 979-8-9888154-4-0

Cover design and interior formatting by FZ Boda
Cover splatter by Don Smith
Image © Hnwinanda

A NOTE TO THE READER

Be aware that some of the stories included in this book contain graphic descriptions of violence, including death, child abduction, necrophilia, murder, and other potentially triggering subjects. If you need help living, coping with trauma or harm, or staying sober, these resources offer support at no cost. Please reach out.

Suicide and Crisis Lifeline

988

The Rape, Abuse & Incest National Network (RAINN)

1-800-656-HOPE

The Trevor Project

1-866-488-7386

Alcoholics Anonymous

aa-intergroup.org/get-help-now

Adult Survivors of Child Abuse (ASCA)

info@ascasupport.org

415-937-1854

DISCLAIMER

On November 17, 1993, performer and musician Brian Warner filed a request to trademark his stage name "Marilyn Manson." Warner received his trademark in 1994 and maintains ownership of "Marilyn Manson," which is defined as "entertainment services; namely, live musical performances of a solo musician and/or musical group; and fan club services." The mark does not identify a specific living individual.

Warner's career was unfairly targeted following the Columbine High School shooting on April 20, 1999. He was blamed for the killings and scapegoated by politicians, religious leaders, entertainment leaders, the media, and other powerful groups. Warner stated in an op-ed that he believed the media itself, society's lax attitude toward violence and guns, and news coverage that glamorized mass murder were actually responsible for Columbine.

In a June 4, 2013 interview with Larry King, Warner shared that he'd taken a legal stance against news outlets who used his trademarked name "Marilyn Manson." He sent cease and desist orders to offenders but did not pursue litigation. Warner said he had been blamed for about 36 school shootings since Columbine.

"Marilyn Manson" is referred to throughout this book. The name is included as a historical artifact from the post-Columbine era and a cultural phenomenon. No trademark infringement is intended.

THIS ONE'S FOR MY LATE
GRANNY, MY QUQU.

Thanks a lot, society, for railroading my ass.

-Aileen Wuornos

CHAPTER ONE

JUNE 17, 1999. Welcome to Yeehaw Junction, Florida. I'm Skeet and I'm gonna be a school shooter when I grow up. I got the idea from Marilyn Manson, who we heard on the radio got three of his ribs removed so he could suck his own dick. Marilyn Manson is also from Florida, which really makes you think. It's June-something, 1999, and today—under the hottest sun you ever felt in your life— me and Cricket stuffed mason jars full of biochemical soil from the Salida Preserve. We'll sell them for $2 a pop outside the farm store.

The soil's from the same land that the U.S. Department of Defense sprayed with killer chemicals back in 1968. We tell people the soil's a wet dream for orange trees because of earthworm leaching. People believe anything you tell them because people don't know shit. Tourists don't. It sounds right and that's all that matters. They get a little souvenir from the Florida back-country on their way to Orlando or the Gulf Coast, slurping triple sludge gulps with extra ice while a rooster chases after a barn cat in the road. They think we're young and dumb and take pity on us, dirty and hot in the street.

This is rancher country and me and Cricket share it with chickens and cows and the contaminated soil and Mr. Ollie at the farm store and our cracker-style house with Trudy and the gang. There's a sinkhole in the prairie and a diner by the Desert Inn that's haunted with ghosts from murdered prostitutes. I know. I've seen them. I've even fucked a few of them.

In the June heat, we left the shoulder of the turnpike to walk through the swamp cabbage in the partial shade. A sign reads Bartow, 62 Miles. I can smell the catfish in the river, all the way from here. I can smell the junkyard, too, all that waste cooking in the sun like fresh armpit. We pull our wagon: me, leading in the front, shirtless and scratching my sunburn; Cricket, in the rear. There's a slab of wood hammered to the side of the wagon and spray painted with 4 SALE FL SUEVINERRS HISTORY. We used to sell navel oranges and strawberries out of the wagon but the farm on Buttermilk Slough caught us basketing their citrus and had a conniption. The owners called the pigs on us and next thing you know their sick, tumored doberman chased me up a cottonwood, all that fruit flying through the air like sugar rockets.

We were drenched in sweat, Cricket and me, more than usual on a day like today. We hustled, eager to eat our cake and blow the survivor kazoo back at the house.

Cricket had been pregnant for years and years and years and one day she was gonna have that baby. Cricket is 43 years old. It's the twenty-eighth anniversary of what the Women & Kids' Domestic Violence Society Lake Okeechobee Chapter called Survivor's Day. Every year, they delivered a sheet cake from Publix with half-assed icing and once even the number of "survivor years" frosted in pink flowers. Cricket loved cake almost as much as she loved a celebration. She'd been fourteen when she became a survivor. She was first rescued by a dairy farmer that got sick and tired of listening to Cricket scream bloody murder because her daddy was rubbing sunscreen up her private parts. Cricket's daddy went to prison for being a pervert and Cricket got a cake every year after that.

"How many years, Skeet?" Cricket said.

Her dark freckles and frumpy, dishwater haircut gave away her real age but she still had the mind of a young girl: ageless, sort of, head stuck in the girls' home, getting fed government cheese and bologna sandwiches. She'd started carrying around a black-and-white picture of Jimmy Stewart in her pants back at the girls' home; told everybody it was her daddy and wasn't he handsome. She still carried the thing to this day. Cricket was alright, a bit of a headcase. But aren't we all? Truth is, Cricket is about as bright as a nickel.

"Twenty-eight years out. Twenty-eight years since the last time you got raped," I said. "Twenty-eight years ago today, you rode saddle in a pig's cruiser and got your own bed at the girly home."

Cricket smiled.

"I hope it's a vanilla cake for Survivor's Day," she said.

"What about chocolate?"

"I like chocolate, too. Maybe vanilla and chocolate cake mixed together." Cricket took a gulp of river water out of the canteen. "What flavor is icing, anyway?"

"Icing-flavor," I said.

The truth is, today is really going to be something special. Survivor's Day was a big deal because Trudy, the oldest of us, took swell sensitive care of Cricket. Cricket was her favorite of the five of us (six, if you counted Jenna's boyfriend, Ziggy). But we hadn't thrown a party since Bam Bam was small enough to suck on Trudy's milkers. Bam Bam was the only one of us to grow inside of Trudy, her real honest-to-God kid, born with a birth certificate and everything.

"Did you know that the mama's heart gets bigger when the baby's growing inside of her? So much love to give, it's no wonder," Cricket said. "I'm glad I survived."

"I am too, Cricket."

It was a mile hike back to Yeehaw Junction and having to pull the wagon, it took us almost an hour. The prairie was to the right, longleaf pines to the left. Heat rash was giving me a wet, slinky feeling in my undershorts. A trucker hauling ass in a fourteen-wheeler honked at us and we pumped our fists in the air back at him. It's nice to get a little recognition once in a blue moon. Some people get recognition their whole lives. Every time they pump their fist, there's somebody watching. Somebody looks and tells you you're doing a great job–keep up the good work. I can count on a closed fist how many times somebody's looked at me.

Yeehaw Junction wasn't no bigger than a few roads hitched together by a couple prairies and a junkyard. No churches. No schoolhouses. No parks or benches or big box stores. No houses except shotgun houses from the 1930s and double wide trailers in better shape than the houses. It was a long way to the Kissimmee Prairie Preserve, but you could get there from here if you took Buttermilk Slough through the wetlands due north. There was a titty bar and barroom where Trudy worked, a fifteen-room inn, a diner called Stickey's, the farm store that belongs to Mr. Ollie, the gas station that's busy all day. If you've got no brains, you can get to Fort Drum by SR-60.

One of the wagon's wheels squeaked the last quarter mile up the road. Cricket and I switched places. She grabbed the wagon handle and hauled it toward her, the jars clinking and falling over, sliding up and down where the rope wasn't tied. Traffic picked up at Jackass Crossing so we couldn't hear the glass knocking together anymore. And when the rusted wheel scraped at the pavement, the wood pummeled and it busted off, rolling into the storm drain.

"Not again," Cricket said.

I grabbed the back corner of the wagon and hiked the rest of the way hunched forward so the other wheels wouldn't have too much work to do. They were already in bad shape. My fingernails were caked in soil, sand, and sticky crabgrass. I wiped my hands off my pants when we crossed the street. The diner patrons were coming out of Stickey's. Cricket shook a jar at somebody.

"Two dollars! DDT sprayed grass from 1955! Own a piece of Florida history today!"

The lady patron pretended not to notice, jumped in her Georgia-plate vehicle and locked the door. I heard it click. Sometimes older fellows on Harley Davidsons got us fast food. Sometimes they even bought a jar of dirt or offered us canned ravioli or canned wieners.

Having no luck at the diner, we hoofed it to the farm store and gas station. They were right next to each other, one and the same place owned by Mr. Ollie who liked us about as much as we tolerated him. The sky was a barrel of sun, bleaching everything in Yeehaw Junction. We left our broken wagon out front by the gas pumps and stacked tires and went inside where the bell on the door jingled, and the people inside were making a fuss watching an Amber Alert on the T.V.

And the search for a missing young girl in Osceola County continues. Heather Studebaker, 11, was last seen in the parking lot at Fort Drum Service Plaza. Here is her sixth-grade school picture. If you have any information, call our tip line at—

"Amber Alert," a patron said, shaking her head, sick of it all. You could tell she didn't like violence by the way she threw a buck at Bobby for a lottery ticket.

Bobby was the clerk. He was Mr. Ollie's nephew or cousin, some family shit like that. The farm store had three shelves of bread and cookies and a big wall of fridges with milk, eggs, and ice. I opened the door and stuck my head inside, tore open the plastic and seized a handful of ice. I rubbed it on my sunburn and under my armpits, then popped in my mouth like chewing gum. I yelled for Cricket to come and cool her cooch, but she was busy flipping through a T.V. Guide with *Star Wars* shit on the front cover. I hate Star Wars.

"I know a lot of kids I'd like to see go missing that never do," Bobby said, sneering at me and Cricket as we moseyed by the candy rack.

"Prayers up, folks," another patron said. "Once they opened the express lane on I-75 outta Hillsborough County, these types of crimes dominoed."

Kidnapped Heather. I had my suspicions about her abduction. That 11-year-old white girl didn't go traipsing into the swamp while her mother took a shit in the public restroom. She'd only been missing for two days but everybody was carrying on. Then again, everybody was always on edge in Yeehaw Junction.

I already knew about the Amber Alert and the girl: the day Heather got snatched, Trudy said she thought Starr might know something because she was talking weird on our landline. Starr is Trudy's girlfriend, lives out in Kissimmee. Trudy also said Starr was crazy for talking about doing crimes on the landline because you didn't know who was listening in on your private conversation.

Starr maybe took her, I said.

You sound like you have a guilty conscience, Trudy had snapped.

"Prayers up," the other patron agreed as Bobby bagged up their soda pop.

"What? What are you staring at?" Bobby said, to me, as soon as the paying customers cleared out.

I took my pretend Jesse James cap gun out of its plastic holster and pointed it at Bobby.

"Bang, bang," I said, pretending to shoot. I retrieved a pack of Newport Golds out of my shorts and lit it up right there. *Alive with Pleasure!*

"Are you alive with pleasure, Bobby?" I said, taking a warm inhale.

Bobby told me to scram.

"Mr. Bobby, guess what. It's my Survivor's Day today," Cricket said.

"Happy Survivor's Day, Cricket."

"And Mr. Bobby, did you know that the placenta comes out during the afterbirth? Say, did you want to join us for my special survivor party? We've got cake."

"Can't. Some of us have to work for a living."

I told Cricket a hundred times not to go around telling people about her Survivor's Day or explaining what it meant. People don't take well to that, especially a guy like Bobby. He'd look at us differently if he knew she'd been raped and had a cake for it every year. Whatever Bobby knew about us he kept to himself.

We left without taking anything except my five-fingered discount on the ice, which seemed fair because it was so hot that nobody even stopped to buy Mr. Ollie's discounted Walt Disney World or SeaWorld tickets he sells out of a stack of tires. Disney World is over sixty miles from here. You got a-ways to go if you stop here to piss.

We walked outside to the front of the farm store. There was a table, chairs, two pumps, "No Diesel," plus a Coca-Cola machine that hasn't worked since the year before last; I suspect something naughty is stored there, but who can say.

"Ollie-ollie-oxen-free, he's kidnapping me!" I said and Mr. Ollie waved, not bothered by the prospect of violence and abduction. Nice fellow. Born to run scams and does it with a servant's heart. "Hi, Mr. Ollie."

"Hi, Mr. Ollie," Cricket said.

"Hi, Skeet. Hi, Cricket. Where's Bam Bam?"

"Filling buckets with hose water 'cuz a hurricane's brewing. I can feel it," Cricket said. She patted her flat belly, licked her index finger, pointed up at the sky to feel the wind. Always doing some redneck shit.

"There is?" Mr. Ollie looked over his sunglasses.

"The cows are lying down."

"Wish I was a cow."

"Don't we all," I said, blowing smoke.

I didn't really want to be a cow in the prairie, though. It was too hot and sometimes it felt like you were swimming through it. Can't apply sunscreen anymore because sunscreen causes cancer. So does the soil. So does the Florida sun. So does fluoride. So does our drinking water, since 1996. The boils on my right hand might be cancer. They're not black yet but they might turn black and then I'm going to hold a lighter to the boils before they spread into the lymph nodes and poop-guts and shoots to my brain. We're all gonna die someday. May as well not think too hard about it.

Mr. Ollie, like his sidekick, Bobby, is a fellow we've known all our lives—at least since my beginning a long time ago, whenever that was. Mr. Ollie wore a sun hat with a bolo sticking out of it that Cricket called his *macaroni*. He didn't have a lot to say. Some of the smartest people don't. It's all in their eyes. Or on their hat. Mr. Ollie liked us even when he didn't. Sometimes we messed things up for him real bad. His breath smelled oniony. He helped locate things for Jenna's dirty market. Jenna, Trudy's other foster kid, got her hands on everything rotten, from crematorium ashes incinerated from a baby to soiled period pads to graphic photographs of car accidents.

Some dick driving a truck with a Jesus fish decal and an action figure Jesus, arms out to the wind hanging off the rear view, laid on his horn because we were standing where he was trying to be.

"Alright, alright—move out the way, you two," Mr. Ollie said. "These are my customers."

Cricket, with a jar in her hand, shook it wildly so the driver could see it.

"Ollie-ollie-oxen-free!" she said. "Two dollars!"

I tossed what was left of the cigarette at the dick in the truck. Clouds of dirt came rising around the three of us. "Come on, motherfucker!"

"Leave it," Mr. Ollie said. "I got something for you, Cricket." He smacked his gums, reaching down between the rows of tires behind him. Whatever the gift was, it was wrapped up in a day's worth of newspaper. "Happy Whatever Day. Open it. Or don't. I don't care."

"For me?" she said.

Cricket tore the paper off, her blue eyes blazing with the intensity of a pelican going after a trout. That girl was so full of light you'd forget sometimes that she was a headcase wearing a sparkly butterfly clip in her hair.

"Skeet, look!"

"What is it?" I said.

"It's a .22 caliber," said Mr. Ollie. "And girls like you need it these days. Look at what's going on down in Fort Drum with that girl missing and all."

"That's lethal," I said, touching the shiny barrel before taking it out of Cricket's hands. What was hers was mine anyway. Everybody knew that. "Whoa, heavy as all hell."

Cricket narrowed her eyes, crinkling her lips. "Mr. Ollie, I don't know. I'm not allowed to play with guns. Trudy said."

Mr. Ollie laughed, looking up at the cloudless day as if he was expecting to see the hurricane Cricket predicted. "Who said anything about playing? Do you play with handguns? No—you *handle* a handgun. Trudy ain't always right."

"Sometimes she is," said Cricket. "This gun is bigger than a baby's size in the first trimester. In the mama, the baby's the size of an orange. This gun is bigger than an orange!"

Mr. Ollie took a swig of his cola. "Okay, you got yourself a .22. Do you know what a 10-10 means? It means don't do nothing stupid with it. After you learn to use it, I'll give you a bullet every week until it's full. Got it?"

Cricket said gently, "Thank you, Mr. Ollie. Can I ask you something?"

"No. Save it. I've got work to do."

He looked at me and grabbed my slippery hand, spit in my palm. "Clean your fingers, boy. You got blood on 'em."

I jolted and jerked my hand back. "Yeah, okay," I said.

There were little specks of dried blood around my boils and in my fingernail beds. Mr. Ollie noticed everything even when we didn't want him to.

CHAPTER TWO

911 Transcript of Ms. Dolores Studebaker
June 14, 1999, 09:34 A.M.
Okeechobee County EOC

911: Police, fire, or medical?

STUDEBAKER: Send everybody! Please! My daughter, she's gone!

911: What's your location?

STUDEBAKER: I'm at a rest stop! Please hurry!

(UNIDENTIFIED WOMAN): Fort (inaudible) Service!

(UNIDENTIFIED MAN): –turnpike!

STUDEBAKER: Fort Drum Service Plaza! Please help me!

911: I have police en route. How old is your daughter, ma'am?

STUDEBAKER: She's 11! Somebody took her! She's not here!

911: Do you know who took your daughter?

STUDEBAKER: Of course not! I went inside the plaza to the bath-room, I came back and she's not here! She's gone!

911: What is your name?

STUDEBAKER: (inaudible)

911: What is your name?

STUDEBAKER: Dolores Studebaker.

911: Dolores, please stay on the line with me. Did anybody see your daughter get into a vehicle or leave with someone?

STUDEBAKER: Everybody in this plaza is looking for her!

(UNIDENTIFIED MAN): Pontiac Firebird got outta here quick when I pulled up to the pump!

911: What color was the Pontiac Firebird?

(UNIDENTIFIED WOMAN): (inaudible)

(UNIDENTIFIED MAN): I think white. No, blue!

911: Dolores, do you know anybody that drives a Pontiac Firebird or a vehicle like it?

STUDEBAKER: No! Oh my God!

911: Give me a description of your daughter. What's her name? What was she wearing?

STUDEBAKER: Jesus, bring her back to me.

911: Ma'am, police are on their way. Stay on the line with me. What is your daughter's name?

STUDEBAKER: She's 11! She's—her name is Heather Elizabeth. She would never just walk off without telling me!

911: And what was Heather wearing?

STUDEBAKER: She's got long hair but she was wearing it up in a ponytail braid, okay? I think. She was in a t-shirt that was white with the Britney Spears singer on it. Everybody here's looking for her!

911: Dolores. I know. Stay on the line with me until police arrive.

STUDEBAKER: I screamed her name! There ain't even anywhere for her to go around here!

911: I know—

(UNIDENTIFIED WOMAN): Here! (inaudible)

STUDEBAKER: I'm going–

911: Dolores?

CALL ENDED AT 09:37 AM

CHAPTER THREE

JUNE 17, 1999. We don't live off the beaten path. We live a mile from the titty bar that sits above Stickey's in the shadows of a beaten-down marquee at a ratty motel. The staircase to the bar is suncracked and the building's stripped of life except for the truck drivers that peel off the road with caffeinated eyes, hauling locked-up consignment. There's an unwelcoming statue of a chainsaw wood cowboy and Native American holding the stripey Florida state flag with "Nation Under God" on an old restaurant sign. *Please Seat Yourself.*

Me and Cricket haven't been welcome in the diner for two years. None of us in Trudy's gang have stepped foot in Stickey's, not even Trudy, despite working upstairs with her titties out and needing hydration every now and then. I got caught taking food from somebody's half-eaten club sandwich and fries plate. I wasn't hungry. I just wanted to take something that didn't belong to me. Jenna got caught, too, after she got a job as a Stickey's waitress. She mouthed off to a Mississippi trucker that grabbed her ass. It's just the way life is sometimes; you're not wanted at the diner downstairs from the titty bar.

We dragged our broken three-wheeled wagon to the stoop, opening the door to a corridor with framed pictures of horses and harpoons and old men in rain slickers holding swordfish lining the dark shotgun staircase. A tarnished frame of Jesus Christ in his cape. The smell of nicotine wrapped around us. Two men played pool in a cloud of cigarette smoke. There's a fish tank with green lights surrounding the bar. "That Smell" by Lynyrd Skynyrd on the jukebox. Old-timer noise.

"There she is," Cricket said, over the music. "Trudy looks so beautiful."

My eyes adjusted to the amber stagelight Trudy moved around in. She looked like she had two fish hanging out of her chest, pushing into her belly. Her areolas looked like the scooped out eyes of a dead fish. Her hair was a rat's nest, tied up, half-assed, half-baked auburn from the sun. The tattoos of gold stars and kissy lips down her spine had all but faded; you couldn't tell what they were anymore other than permanent. She rubbed her fat, flappy titties and pretended there was smoke blowing out of each one.

"Knock on wood and maybe you'll get your answer!" she hollered to the truckers playing pool and whistling through their smokes.

Then something happened that I couldn't explain. I'll tell you right now that Cricket missed the whole thing because she was giggling at Trudy, so she couldn't explain it either.

The electricity flickered and across the room, a man appeared out of thin air. I don't know who he was. Never saw him before. He wore a black trench coat and small black eyeglasses. Even at a distance I spotted his quivering jowl and grim eyes. I could hear him over the music, over the bar noise, whispering. His lips moved; I was the only one his words reached.

"Radium and lead in youngblood's head. Everything goes to hell," he hissed.

I gave him a sharp look, having felt something like breath on the back of my neck. I turned around. How had he gotten past me? The man in black took a hard look at me before he staggered away, his trench coat dragging behind him as he disappeared through the batwing doors.

Radium and lead in youngblood's head. Everything goes to hell.

A lot of things these days don't make sense. It didn't make sense that the man in black wore a trench coat in 92-degree summer temperature.

But Florida had a way of playing tricks on you.

A half hour later, me, Cricket, and Trudy walked home. She wore a baggy t-shirt from Daytona Beach '86 that said *Suns Out Buns Out!* Her crazy hair was pulled back in a scrunchie. Cricket still had the gun in her pants. I dragged the wagon. The rusted wheels held strong. The jars jangled and Trudy snapped at me, told me to flip them on their sides so they'd quit making all that racket. She was getting a headache.

We walked on the grass next to the shoulder of the road, baking in the heat. To the right of us were longleaf pines and toothy bismarcks and to the left, across the road, was where Buttermilk Slough divided the prairie, cows everywhere. It wasn't uncommon to see somebody in a marked van from the University of Florida with their cameras and vials and orange vests, testing the waters for poison. Up from there was the St. John's River and it went all the way to the dick-looking panhandle, to Apalachicola, over the wetlands to grandmother's house we go.

"Who do you think that man was at the bar?" I said, licking the sweat off my lip.

"What man?" Trudy said.

"He had on a trench coat; said some nonsense."

"What did he say?"

"Don't remember."

"Liar," said Trudy. "If you think there's a cop watching me, you gotta fucking tell me. Don't play with me."

I shrugged. "Who's playing?"

Cricket skipped ahead of us to the staggerbush at the end of the street. There was a concrete slab in the ground that collected ditchwater and a wood pile that was usually littered with trash thrown by bottleneck tourists. Cricket liked to look for skunks there but they didn't come out until nighttime.

"It wasn't no pig," I said.

"Then what, a pervert?"

"No pervert neither." I picked up a small rock and threw it at a sports car going eighty down our street. "Asshole!"

Trudy looked over her shoulder. "Walk faster."

"Why?"

"Just do what I fucking tell you."

What I knew about Trudy wasn't much and you don't know what you don't know. She was fifty-one, fifty-two, I guess. She never told me where she was born and I took that to mean she was from Yeehaw Junction. I didn't know if she had any brothers or sisters or a mom or a dad, or anyone at all. She'd never done real time except for a hit-and-run charge: she got off on a battered housewife defense and was processed to a first timers' program for nonviolent offenders. Only fourteen months probation and she passed with flying colors. And she didn't even need to perform community service because we were her community service.

Trudy was our guardian—there was me, Skeet (12), Cricket (43), Macon (17), Jenna (16), and Bam Bam (6). Bam Bam was the only kid that grew up in Trudy's cooter and came out the back, or anyhow that's how Trudy told the story. Bam Bam was Trudy's real blood and bone, but he was still just another mouth to feed and another dependent to claim on Trudy's forms. When Bam Bam had turned five, WIC stopped faster than a smashed possum on I-95. Some birthday.

The first of the month was payday. Money wasn't coming out of Trudy's ass like Bam Bam had, but every month checks came in the mail addressed to Trudy Hooper. We were welfare kings and every bigwig in the nation hated us for it. Said so in the paperwork. Food stamps came in an envelope on the first, too. Cricket got a check from the Southern Adults with Developmental Disabilities, but Trudy spent the money. My favorite part about the first of the month was a special stipend for child rape survivors. Cricket collected those handouts like they were daisies. There was always somebody handing out gifts to somebody that got raped. Just look at the yearly cake.

Real money was different, dirtier. We made ends meet doing rotten things. Bad things. Things Marilyn Manson might do while recruiting kids to the Trench Coat Mafia.

On top of welfare and dancing at the titty bar, Trudy made extra cash doing specialty modeling. She posed next to dead bodies in lacy black underwear with "slut" embroidered on her ass. She had friends, people she knew, and they saw to it that overdoses or homicides went unreported for a few hours so Trudy could pose with them. Suicides, old and young. Infants at the hospital morgue. Like I said, Trudy knew folks.

Jenna took the rotten pictures and Ziggy sold them to special scumbags that found our family business in a sticky layer of the world wide web. We sent the items postal mail or handed them off at a busy strip mall, the meet-up arranged in a pay phone call. There's a funny rotten business for everything. Sometimes you just have to know where to look.

I was special, not rotten. My story started in a trash can at Jacksonville General Hospital in the women's emergency restroom. I was only a couple of hours old when Trudy, working custodial at the time, scooped me up. I was tangled up in plastic trash and discarded paper towels, but she took me home. I'd been her golden boy. The one from the mire. The muck stuck to me and I stayed muddy. My teeth grew in with gaps, short choppy hair, no pigment in my eyes either. I was the boy without any color in his eyes.

"Can I ask you something?" I said to Trudy. I hocked a loogie on the pavement. "Starr, she took off last week. No note or nothin'."

"What's your point?"

"Just thinking, is all. If she don't come back, we don't got a car to get around."

"What do you need a car for?" Trudy said. "Where have you got to go?"

"No place. But sometimes me and Jenna take the camcorder to the high school in Kissimmee to film the bomb threat walk-outs and fights. It's too hot to hitchhike."

Trudy reached into my shorts pocket. "Gimme a cigarette."

"I think we need a car."

"You're gonna tell me what we need now? Ziggy's got wheels. Use your head for once." Trudy exhaled the smoke as she waved back to Cricket, who was sniffing the wood pile for skunk piss. "Come on, baby, let's go home!"

"Starr brings us Kentucky Fried Chicken. The combo comes with a drink."

"What—you got a crush on her or some shit? Don't soil your britches over it," Trudy said.

Cricket joined us the rest of the walk home, affectionately pawing at Trudy who doted on her because it was Survivor's Day. She had a story like mine, Cricket did, except most of it we had to piece together ourselves. Her memory got all fogged from when she was in the girls' home. Trudy found Cricket twenty years ago out in a Sears Tire Center. She'd come in off the street and was a stinking mess, picking through pocket change to afford a candy bar.

"Anybody following us?"

I looked over my shoulder. "Nobody."

Home came into view just as the wagon got heavier. Pulling that handle, another wheel in front was about to pop off. We were surrounded by white cracker houses and double-wides. In our yard, there was a swing set and inflatable swimming pool that fills with leaves after it rains. Chickens ran amok and there was buckshot in the grass.

"Who's my little survivor?" Trudy said.

Cricket squeezed Trudy's ribcage, looking as gleeful as I'd ever seen her. "I am."

"That's right. How many years?"

"Twenty-eight. And you know what? Twenty-eight years is equal to eighty-four trimesters in 336 months." Cricket counted on her fingers. "That's over thirty-seven pregnancies!"

"Uh-huh, good girl."

"I did it."

"You sure did. You got out of that man's fist, told him who you are and what you're made of."

"Is there cake?"

"You bet," Trudy said. "Survivor girls get their cake and eat it too."

The grass was wet. Bam Bam had left the hose water on and then climbed up the oak tree. He brandished a broken ceiling fan blade. Trudy pitched a fit. The minute she started yelling, her natural son fished a plastic Monica Lewinsky mask out of the tree branches. He slid the mask over his face and peered down at us from the oak. I left the wagon in the grass, flashing him the finger. I picked up the hose and gulped.

"Go wet your feet and come inside," Trudy called. "It's a hot one."

The open Florida-room door slammed shut, *The Fresh Prince of Bel-Air* playing on the T.V. Bam Bam jumped down from the tree, soaked his feet with hose water, and followed me inside to the pigpen. Trudy snatched the mask off Bam Bam. These days, Trudy wore it all the time for her rotten necro videos.

"And where the fuck is Macon on a day like today?" Trudy said, cigarette in her mouth, the red-lipped, bushy-haired Lewinsky mask under her armpit. "I told him to come home for cake."

Jenna was curled up in Ziggy's lap on the loveseat. The box fan snapped as it whirled in front of them, blowing her curls. She beamed at Cricket, who lit up at her question: "Did you make a million on Survivor's Day?"

"You know I didn't. Made $11 on my jars and Skeet made $6 on his jars."

"Cake's in the fridge," Ziggy said, not taking his eyes off Will Smith on the T.V.

I couldn't blame him. I loved Will Smith. He was the greatest American actor living today.

We had four rusted shopping carts from the nearest Winn-Dixie wedged between three lawn chairs and the loveseat. Clothes in piles with empty food packages and 99-cent store soda cans and stacked phone books under an empty bird cage. A pregnant rat scurried out from behind the T.V. with a holey barnacle growing out of its back; it only came out during daylight. There were old McDonald's fountain drinks with ants crawling up the straws, and a pink baby carriage filled with tubes of 99-cent hair dye that the rat used to give birth or shit into.

I knelt down to the 99-cent box hair dye to see if the rat had slurped up the rest of the color. (Not yet.)

The T.V. had a VCR but we only watched MTV, *The Fresh Prince of Bel-Air*, and *Married...With Children*. Lately, all that MTV played was a commercial for Woodstock '99 in New York. Marilyn Manson was gonna be there but I don't got a clue where New York is.

If you kept the lights turned on at home, you didn't have to see the cockroaches spill out of old cereal boxes and dry linens and up the nicotine walls. Sometimes we caught 'em in the cheese cracker box but the crackers are still good. You just give it a shake and they fly off. We had a centerfold of Will Smith hanging on the wall. We had potatoes under the sink with fungus that's spread into the plaster and curled fungi vined on the handle. Bathtub didn't work. It was filled with bathroom trash and moldy towels from when we had a pipe burst two years ago. We also kept cat litter in there for making fireworks. The hot water didn't work. I'm not sure it ever did. There was a permeating damp heat despite the air conditioning unit that sat in the window, coated in termite dust. We had a phone in the wall and it worked when the bill was paid. We never replaced lightbulbs. When the bulb burned out, we just let it be dark.

"Watch where you're going with that thing," Trudy snapped her fingers at Bam Bam, who was holding the ceiling fan blade. "Jeez Louise, you wanna spend Survivor Day in the E.R. getting stitches in your tongue or eating cake?"

"Cake," said Bam Bam dejectedly.

We gathered around the yellow kitchen countertop to see the Survivor Cake. It was vanilla this year with buttercream icing and pink roses. In the center, a folded paper stuck out the top that said *You Did It!*

Cricket puffed into the survivor kazoo.

"There's not any candles to blow out," Cricket said.

"Hold your horses, girl, Jesus!" Trudy said. "Macon's not getting any because he couldn't be bothered to show up and celebrate."

I arranged Cricket's white birthday candles into a smiley face, striking a match to light them. She made her wish and fingered the pink roses up out of the icing and into her mouth as I scooped fat slices onto paper plates for everybody. Cricket mostly just ate the topping. After eating cake, me and Bam Bam took swigs of red flavor Nyquil and from the loveseat I sang "Gettin' Jiggy Wit It" from Will Smith's new CD. Trudy didn't like a lot of noise but she said freedom of speech went farther than headaches and I could do it until it got dark, because it was just about dark then.

While I sang the na-na-na-na-na-na's, shirtless and barefoot, feeling the Nyquil's warmth come over me, I watched Trudy savor the last drag of her cigarette. She looked out the window blinds in the Florida-room, looking at somebody or something. Maybe nothing at all.

There was a time our gang all shaved our heads to make it look like we had cancer. Leukemia. The most common disease for kids. We took to the streets, asking for money for cancer treatment outside the children's hospital at the traffic light. Some knew we were full of shit. Some people prayed over us with the Holy Spirit. Jenna's hair had grown down to her ass since then, so curly it got stuck in her bracelets and she bitched about that. She had freckles like Cricket had freckles. She'd been dating Ziggy since she was thirteen, over three years.

"Survivin' and thrivin'," Jenna said. "Tell Cricket she's good shit, Ziggy."

"She's good shit, Ziggy," he said, not taking his eyes off the T.V.

Cricket sat in a heap of clothes, working on her second slice of cake. "I'm Mama's survivor girl."

Trudy scowled. "What did I tell you about calling me 'Mama?' Is that what I am to you? A *mom*? Not Trudy, but a fucking mama?"

Jenna laughed. "You on the rag? Leave that girl alone."

"Aw, lighten up," I said. "Sometimes Cricket forgets."

Cricket, smarter than some of us kids gave her credit for, changed the subject. She patted her belly one-handed, licking the icing off the top of her cake slice.

"Sorry, Trudy," she said. "I'm practicing for my little one."

"Well, practice makes perfect when you don't got any sense. But keep it to yourself."

"Okay, Trudy."

Ziggy snickered, shaking his head at the whole ordeal. He had long, greasy black hair that hung past his shoulders, a tribal tat on his forearm, and Pontius Pilate on his chest.

"So, what's its name gonna be?" Ziggy asked.

"I haven't decided," said Cricket.

"'Mary' is nice," offered Trudy.

"No good," I said. "God got Mary pregnant when she was just a little girl. Didn't ask her or nothing. That's rape and pedophilia in one. It makes you think."

"Maybe Mary's a survivor like me," Cricket smiled. "I wish the baby would come today. That would be fun. A baby on Survivor's Day."

Jenna shook her head, fanning herself with the crumbly paper plate because the air conditioner wasn't cutting it these days. "You're something else. She's something else. You know that, Trudy?" She looked over at Trudy, who was staring out the window at the blackest night.

"Uh-huh."

Later that night, Macon came home and fought with Trudy. He helped himself to a can of franks and beans and a paper cup of grape Kool-Aid. He'd promised to get me the blueprints to a middle school in Kissimmee for my school shooting practice. He was the only one of us that had ever been enrolled in school. Attended through eighth grade. He had a library card, too, which was good for sneaking blueprints.

Trudy asked him about a paycheck for some slum job he got and if he wanted suckerpunched for not sharing it, and Macon said he didn't care, he just wanted everybody to shut the fuck up because he had some news to share.

Macon was seventeen, on the verge of turning eighteen. He was the biggest dickwad scumbag in Yeehaw Junction, maybe in all of fucking Florida. When he turned eighteen, it meant even less welfare in our mouths. Less money for Trudy. More shifts at the titty bar and more rotten photos.

"Hey," I whispered. "Did you get my blueprints?"

"I got something else," he said.

"What's that mean?"

"It means what I said, fuckface," Macon said, his triple chin looking like a second mouth that was about to eat me for dinner. Spiky hair to cut me with. "Look."

He unfolded a flier.

MISSING IN OSCEOLA COUNTY
HEATHER ELIZABETH STUDEBAKER
LAST SEEN: JUNE 15, 1999 IN FORT DRUM
DATE OF BIRTH: APRIL 4, 1988
SEX: FEMALE
RACE: CAUCASIAN
EYES: BROWN
HAIR: DARK BLONDE
REWARD - $100,000

None of us bickered about this because there was nothing to bicker about. Well-rounded, smiling, normal white girls went missing in other towns but Kidnapped Heather had vanished on our turf, or, at the very least, near it. Nobody ever gets too far from where they disappear, even dirty rotten girls that had it coming. You had your needle in a haystack, but someone as un-rotten and tame as Heather wouldn't know how to do anything except what her kidnappers told her. We'd find her and collect the reward money.

"Does it matter if she's dead or alive?" Jenna asked. "Because if we find her body in the creek and she's swimming in her own blood, naked, conked on the head—what then? I'm not wasting my time in this heat."

"First of all, why don't you lower your voice a bit so the dumb-fuck neighbors ain't in our business?" Trudy said. "That girl's parents, the media, the piggies, they just want a body. Dead or alive, fucked or not, doesn't matter a hair. They just want the dirty details."

A reward of $100,000 was no welfare check. More like a lottery ticket. Sure, the whole state was looking for that eleven-year-old girl, but those people looking weren't us. They didn't know how to find the dirty rotten places where kids went missing. We did. We were rotten people and we came from a rotten place.

While Cricket showed everybody her handgun, talking about her allowance of a bullet a week, I walked out in a Nyquil coma to the porch. No light, no traffic, no people. Chickens. I heard a rhythmic buzzing. I could hear Cricket blowing the kazoo. In the left corner of the porch rafters, wasps had built a nest. I stuck my head as close as possible to the rafters, to show the wasps how near I could get to them without getting stung. It was pretty fucking close.

CHAPTER FOUR

YOUTUBE CHANNEL: "STRANGE AND UNUSUAL FLORIDA"
EPISODE IV

PUBLISHED BY USER: January 14, 2010

Hey, everybody, and welcome back to my YouTube channel. I'm Craig and today I'm going to be talking about one of Florida's biggest secrets–Yeehaw Junction. Let's get into it.

Yeehaw Junction is located in Florida's watershed, south-central between Lake Okeechobee and Orlando in Osceola County. It's a town that stretches less than two miles with a population of less than two hundred, accessible from SR-60 and the Florida Turnpike. The nearest coast is Vero Beach, forty miles east. During its railroad heyday in the first half of the 20th century, the town was better known as "Jackass Junction." It wasn't until after the installation of the Florida Turnpike that Jackass Junction was more appropriately renamed to "Yeehaw Junction," and the town became a tourist trap staple between major Florida attractions, farmland, and theme parks.

But Florida isn't just beaches, swamps, and manatees. It has its secrets, too. DDT, formally known as dichloro-diphenyl-trichloroethane, a federally produced incesticide that was once thought to eliminate common diseases, is still showing up in Yeehaw Junction's soils and water basin. Banned in 1972 and now considered a deadly contaminant, the land and its population were exposed to high amounts of DDT, due to the weekly "special sprayer vehicles" that engulfed most of the U.S. in clouds of the chemical. (Commercials once advertised DDT's slogan: *So safe you can eat it!*)

From October 31 to December 1, 1968, Yeehaw Junction and its unsuspecting residents were included in a government experiment called Project 112. A cancer-causing agent coined "Agent X" was sprayed over the prairie by a U.S. Air Force fighter jet to determine which spores kill crops. Depending on its effectiveness, the same biochemical weapon would be used to bomb Soviet wheat fields. These experiments were kept secret from Yeehaw Junction's residents and the State of Florida. The cancer-causing weapons systems include but are not limited to stem rust, oxide, and chloroform. A radioactive bacteria was also scheduled to be released into the air in 1969 by the same military fighter craft, but that project was discontinued at the last minute.

Biochemical warfare wasn't the only discontinued government objective in Yeehaw Junction.

In 1986, Florida's penal system was over the legal maximum capacity of prisoners. The Corrections Department of Florida devised a plan to convert and operate Yeehaw Junction's motel and diner into an 1100-inmate prison. The citrus groves would be burned to the ground and the prison expanded. Yeehaw Junction's diner, Stickey's—a regular pitstop for truckers and tourists alike— would permanently close. The closest prison at the time was the

Okeechobee Correctional Institution, a half hour south of Osceola County. However, the zoning permits were never obtained and the plan was dismissed by 1990.

During an active hurricane season in 1993, Yeehaw Junction found itself included in a statewide epidemic where children developed a rare, inflammatory disease called Skeeter Syndrome. Skeeter Syndrome, at the time of the 1993 outbreak, was only reported in Louisiana and Florida. It's a rare reaction to a mosquito's saliva. Anybody from the South can tell you that mosquitoes thrive in warm, damp environments. During a brief investigation of what was causing the buggy outbreak by the University of Florida, water pollutants became a bigger part of Florida's health reports.

Water pollutants have contributed to Florida's dysfunctional reputation. 90 percent of Florida's tap water comes from the Florida Aquifer, which supplies Florida, Georgia, Alabama, and South Carolina with drinking water. There have been over 39 incidents of brain-eating amoeba (*Naegleria fowleri*) in Florida's waters since 1980, including an alleged incident at a Disney World theme park that resulted in the death of a child and the alleged permanent closing of said park, Discovery Island. The Safe Drinking Water Act was first established in Florida in 1974 but hasn't been updated since 1996. The following pollutants exceeded the EPA's legal limit in Florida's water supply as of June 2009.

CHLOROFORM

CYANIDE

MERCURY

TEMIK

TRICHLOROETHYLENE

RADIUM-226

RADIUM-228

LEAD

Benzene

Tetrachloroethylene

Trichlorethylene

Nitrate

Metolachlor (weed killer)

Vinyl chloride

Ethylene dibromide

Radon

Freon

Nitrite

Traces of uranium

Traces of manure

Traces of algae blooms

Alpha

Heptachlor epoxide

Bromoform

Dibromochloromethane

Toluene

Cadmium

Methyl Tert Butyl Ether (MTBE)

Phosphorus

Florida was ranked #1 in the nation for the worst drinking water due to these unregulated chemicals, thanks to weak federal standards, mismanaged pollution, and poor stormwater management. Florida's naturally flat topography allows ample opportunity for pollutants to stick around and slowly dissolve.

And guess what, subscribers? Yeehaw Junction has some mysterious and violent history, too. But you'll have to wait for the next episode of Strange and Unusual Florida to find out. Like and subscribe!

CHAPTER FIVE

JUNE 20, 1999. Life can sure be funny. The fellow that murdered John Lennon with a .38 special lived outside bumfuck Florida in Decatur most of his miserable life. A real Southerner. His name was Mark David Chapman and he was the number one Beatles fan in the whole wide world.

Chapman waited with a gaggle of Beatles fans in the cold and snow in New York City for three fucking days in 1980 waiting to meet John. On the first day, he chickened out. On the second day, he chickened out again. And on the third day, he got the Beatle's autograph and had his picture taken with John before blowing him to bits with five bullets to the chest. All those screaming fans clutching their records, sprayed with John Lennon's blood. Not one fan had the balls to save their idol that day. Nobody did a goddamn thing but ran for their lives. It makes you think.

Marilyn Manson hasn't been murdered by his biggest fan. I hope he never will be. I know I'd take a bullet for that man because I'm not a fake fan.

I started thinking about important stuff like that at sunup on the day the media demanded Heather Studebaker's safe return on the news. "Hope 4 Heather" was the tagline they ran with. They paraded for the missing girl like it was the 4th of July, except with less fireworks. Looking for a child's body brought out togetherness and patriotism, flowers and Beanie Babies, American flags, tears, big hugs, school assemblies, and sermons. News footage flickered through photographs of other lost children playing sports and smiling maniacally in family portraits. Everyone asked the same stupid question: *How Could This Happen?*

The six of us left for Kidnapped Heather's organized search and rescue. I stuffed my Jesse James cap gun in my camo shorts and slabbed on deodorant because Trudy said I reeked and nobody wanted to sniff it.

We left Bam Bam in a deep Nyquil slumber. Finally, he had the mattress all to himself, sprawled out like he owned the place. (All of us shared a bed except for Trudy, that's got her own mattress she fucks Starr on.) Bam Bam was a whiz. He knew not to look out the windows or open the door for anybody that came knocking, don't tell nobody nothing, especially not your name or what the secret family word is. (It's "Ollie-Ollie-Oxen-Free.")

We hoofed it in the morning dark into the stinky belly of Salida Preserve off I-60. Pigs in cruisers had their lights flashing. Orange cones bordered the access road off from the highway.

"Fix your face, boy—frown. That's more like it," Trudy told me.

Down the dirt path, the top of a barn was outlined by a long row of slash pines behind it, and the sky was almost orange. A hundred volunteers gathered in tents and a reporter sidestepped brown muck in high heels and stuck her big microphone in people's faces. The pigs stayed in their cruisers. Crying grown-ups milled around in baggy *Have You Seen Me?* shirts. Volunteers distributed a stack of fliers to hand out at strip malls and movie theaters and parks.

The best part about all of this was the tent for food and drinks. Hot breakfast from McDonald's, chicken and biscuits and gravy from Kentucky Fried Chicken, donuts from Winn-Dixie, juice by the gallon, soda, coffee, milk, and a big ass bucket of ice that could have filled a timber trailer. Most of the other volunteers were older than Moses, but there were middle-aged do-gooders and church people under the tent flap, too. Their earnestness, mixed with the scent of jelly donuts and fried chicken, made me despise grown-ups' bullshit even more. They stuffed their faces, the old people. They flapped their jaws. Talking about the chicken. Eating the chicken. Then talking about the girl some more.

I went into the porta-toilet and watched the other searchers from between the gray slats as I held my dick. I wondered. Do you still have your cup of joe in the morning when a local girl goes missing? Do you wait to drink it until after you've already looked for the body? Do you nurse your coffee and then look? Do you bother with prayer? Do you velcro your shoes and feed the cat?

It makes you think.

Kidnapped Heather's mother showed up in an unmarked van with T.V. reporters at her heels. She was overdressed for the weather. I'd seen too much of her face on T.V. lately, and although I thought Dolores Studebaker was as innocent as a dead nun turned angel, you never can say. I didn't think you could trust the polygraph, fingerprints, T.V. interviews. People could do a crying song-and-dance anytime and anywhere you looked. Fuck, Dolores probably cried herself to sleep the night before-that is, if she got any sleep at all.

"That little bitch's mom showed up," Jenna gestured.

"I see her," Trudy said. "Don't stare."

As I raked through the country biscuits, a kind-faced woman with small eyeglasses and a pointy chin separated everybody into four groups. She skirted around a table, her hairline already beaded in sweat, and waved me and the rest of the gang over with a bunch of busybody volunteers and Dolores, too. The facilitators insisted we "prevent child abduction" by getting our pictures taken and sticking our fingers in black powder.

Trudy told us to put a sock in it before we fussed: they did it in case something happened to us on the hike.

The facilitators passed out bright orange search and rescue vests that didn't tie or button-snap. I decided right then and there I'd keep mine forever. I'd always wanted one. I could get away with anything in this outfit. I traded mine with Trudy that needed more room because of her tits and smoothed down the smaller one she gave me. I felt like Jesse James, or Mark David Chapman, or like the guy that knew what happened to Kidnapped Heather and was taking everybody for a ride.

"Children under fourteen are generally not allowed to volunteer," said the pointy-nosed woman.

"We're not children, missy," Cricket snapped.

"That's fine. Most of you are Heather's peers and are probably dealing with some very big emotions right now," the lady said. "Everyone, I'm Joyce Smith. I'm a non-profit facilitator with Our Children Forever. I'll be your guide today. That gentleman over there, that's Ronny Esposito. He works with me.

"You folks are the Yeehaw Junction group. This is our grid map—it shows all walkability of today's search. We'll cover Yeehaw Junction to Fort Drum today on foot, in these X'd areas. We start promptly at 7:45 a.m. and go until about 8:oo p.m. tonight. There'll be plenty of food and drinks available throughout the day and we encourage you to take frequent breaks."

"Is there gonna be more Kentucky Fried Chicken?" I said, and Trudy shot me a look. Her patience was being tested.

"I believe there will be, son," Joyce said. "We're so thankful for today's food donations."

"I like the biscuits and gravy," said Cricket. "At eighteen weeks, a baby inside of its mama is the size of a bell pepper, which is the same size as a Kentucky Fried Chicken biscuit."

"Last but not least," Joyce said. "Fliers. Our agency has printed twenty-five thousand of these to cover over seventy counties from here to Georgia, and, God willing, we'll print more as needed. Telephone poles, trees, school fences, store shop doors and windows: wherever there's a business, wherever there's a space, let them know who we are and what we're doing. Don't be shy with the fliers. Let them know Heather Studebaker's name. Hope 4 Heather."

I looked around at the do-gooder volunteers, glared at Jenna, gave Ziggy the bird. Good Samaritans in the summer heat thinking they were making a difference. Here it was: some bullshit. I could smell it—their sweat, their somber moods. Their prayers were bone dry. Not real fans of Kidnapped Heather. Instead, the crowd was re-evaluating having come out to the swamp when the temperature was already in the upper 8os. They were grateful it hadn't been their kid that disappeared into thin air, never to be seen again. Maybe into some seedy man's car. Maybe into the mouth of a hungry alligator. Deep down, these people were scumbags and hags, happy there was nothing to worry about except turning on the news at night and seeing what hadn't happened to them—not this time. This time, they got away.

The manhunt started at the preserve. We walked through infinite tall grass and sawed palmetto as the yellow sun struck us with no mercy. I joined the other volunteers in screaming her name.

"Hea-ther!"

People got on their hands and knees in the dirt to sift for clues, pawing the fringed bachelor's buttons in patches near ant hills.

"Hea-ther!"

Looking down at purple fringes, five steps behind Cricket, I went back and crushed the wildflowers with my hightops. I didn't want to see anything beautiful.

Long-horned grasshoppers the size of my hand flickered in the grass, trilling, exploding into noise the closer we got to a gloomy pothole at the far, four-mile mark in Salida. The groundwater glinted golden in the sun. There was some ruckus from the volunteers. Somebody–an old fellow in fucking chinos–found something on the surface of the black water, loaded at its sunken edges with yellowed weeds. Joyce Smith and Ronny Esposito, the head go-getters, ran to the pothole. Everybody crowded around. I pushed to the front, going between people's legs. It was only a bird, though, its head like straw, marble eyes, its red talons kicking out of the broom of its feathers. I resisted the urge to take it with me.

So, we kept searching.

"Hea-ther!"

Joyce Smith blew a whistle and directed us to spread out as much as possible. We'd cover more ground that way. There were miles to go.

I fucked around and fished my hand into a mud puddle in a hole in the ground. Fingers closed around mine. I gasped, catching the reflection of a man in black in the gloomy water. It was the stranger from the titty bar. He knelt across from me in the tall grass with his hand grasping mine under the water. His grip was strong and he stared a dagger into me as if to declare me guilty. His jowl quivered. I could see he was missing a tooth in the small gap between his shaking lips.

He said to me, "Radium and lead in youngblood's head. Everything goes to hell."

"Who the fuck are you?" I fumbled to pull out the Jesse James cap gun.

He let go of my hand and slinked off, his trenchcoat trailing behind him as if a great wind would pick it up and he'd fly away.

"Creep," I said.

We walked forever like doomed children on a Crusade. We arrived at the drainage that blended into Buttermilk Slough. Joyce Smith took a headcount. Cricket, being Cricket, got carried away talking to the birds. Trudy made her stand close as we walked beneath a canopy of slash pine trees, a florid green rising around us, and then just as fast, turning back into tallgrass and open rancher country. From time to time, Dolores Studebaker broke into tears as she called her daughter's name. I think she was starting to lose her voice from all that misery and desperation. We walked under a live oak tree to get a little shade. Eventually, the slash pines became rows of bleached frangipani and we returned to a dirt road.

"Hea-ther!"

Some of the old timer volunteers spray painted the areas we'd covered in pink Xs. Kind of like the ones on Cricket's survivor birthday cake. Ronny Esposito passed out Gatorades and I gulped red flavor and blue flavor until my tongue turned purple. Trudy had run out of steam by lunchtime. We'd already hiked all morning. She couldn't believe none of us found anything yet. Not one limb, not one hair tie, not one trace of blood.

After lunch at the slough, after the Kentucky Fried Chicken and Pizza Hut got delivered and we were all properly fed, we crossed to the west side of where Salida ran to Yeehaw Junction and the prairie smashed its marsh against the turnpike. It was time to get wet. At least up to our knees and hips, depending on how tall you were born.

The marsh stunk. An abductor would have to be stupid to drag Heather through here. Shadows of hardwood hammocked the water. Palmettos for days. Watching the old people balance using umbrellas and trekking poles as they pulled back palmettos and swamp cabbage to have a look like it was somebody's undercarriage, was one of the funniest things I'd ever seen in my life. Ziggy stifled a laugh by biting onto Jenna's hand. She snatched it back, smacking him. Told him to keep it to himself. I thought about the divers on pontoons in neighboring lakes in Central Florida. Had anybody found her yet? I wondered. No. But she had to be close. Even if she ran away, she couldn't have gone too far.

"Hea-ther!"

The tree shadows fell on us as we traipsed out of the swamp and onto the road toward Chicken Hill, where the junkyard was. It wasn't a hill. It was flat as the rest of the state, like if Florida was turned into a pancake and set to cool; we called it "Chicken Hill" because of all the chickens running out of the joint.

Mr. Ollie owned Chicken Hill like he also owned the gas station and the farm store. We played there all the time, shooting soda cans out of box trucks and over milk crates. It was three acres and dangerous because of the crusher pile, according to Mr. Ollie, but everything was dangerous in Florida, even home.

Joyce Smith gave us the 411 on pulling the place apart looking for this girl. Of course, what Joyce Smith didn't realize was that if we found Kidnapped Heather in the junkyard that meant that Mr. Ollie did it, and, well, maybe he did. Sometimes people turned. Sometimes people go crazy. Sometimes people go mad.

"Hea-ther!"

The sun shone brightly off the rusted rims of a 1979 Bronco in the left corner entrance of Chicken Hill. Everybody spread out. Some people readied themselves to climb over junk. Old hags looked in old tires. There was an old Packard Thunderbolt and pulled-apart farm trucks heaved in the grass, stacks of trailer awnings and short bed Dodges, milk crates, trash from the farm store. The crusher pile was a mountain, and the piston in the machine looked like a robot weathered by a storm. I hated that thing but I wasn't afraid of it.

I picked up the slack and poked at everything that the old people from St. Cloud decided not to rummage through—broken road signs, a raccoon carcass. I called out that girl's name like there was no tomorrow.

"Skeet, look!" Cricket nearly pissed her britches when she saw a black cat with mangy fur and beady eyes run up a tree. She chased it, trying to grab its tail. "Come here, kitty-kitty!"

I was distracted, then. A girl from our group introduced herself to me near the rear of the piston. She was freckly and small all over. She wore a visor on top of her ponytail: *Girls Swim Team '98*.

"I'm Olivia."

"What's up?"

"So," she said. "How do you know Heather?"

I shrugged. "Real men help out—know what I'm saying?"

"I know," Olivia said.

She lifted a plank of wood, flipping it hard in the grass. Her pinched expression braced for a critter to scamper out of the pile. She didn't even bother with the gloves that were handed out to us. Sawdust rose from the pile like spores. She dusted her hands off.

"We went to school together," she said.

"You're friends?"

"Sort of. She's in all my classes."

Olivia climbed on top of an old office chair, heaving her body weight into the passenger door of a farm truck. She told me to watch out for wasps. She looked in the back seat and sighed when she didn't see anything. She opened the glove compartment. Then, she joined me back on the ground and we climbed up a hill of dead engines and old wood furniture, stepping on dirty refrigerators and onto the half-crushed stairs to the old guard house.

"What school do you go to?" she asked.

"Don't."

"Did you drop out? My mom would kill me."

"Didn't have to," I said. "Never went."

Olivia must have been satisfied with that answer because she didn't ask me anything else. We jumped off the broken stairs and refrigerator and into the grass, walking alongside the fence.

"I talked to a detective yesterday," Olivia said. "They asked me a lot of questions."

"What kind of questions?"

"If Heather ever talked about running away or if she got in trouble at school. Stuff like that."

"You think she ran away?"

"Hell no," Olivia said. "I think she was grabbed by a grabber. It's just ... weird. Like, she was a good kid. Do you think bad things happen to good people?"

"Bad stuff happens all the time. Just look at John Lennon," I said.

"Who?"

"You wouldn't get it." I took out a cigarette, lit it there in the shade. "Be happy the grabber didn't grab you. You might be next."

"What?"

"Sometimes these things have patterns. People that hurt little kids, they sign up to volunteer for stuff like this all the time. They blend in." I shrugged, offering her a smoke. "It makes you think."

Olivia took the cigarette and inhaled. I could tell by the careful way she put it to her lips, she hadn't done it before. "It does."

Chicken Hill took the rest of the day to search, top to bottom. We even combed the grass, every inch pulled apart and lifted and shouted into only to hear our own voices echoing back at us. Some of the milk crates had tadpoles floating in old rainwater. Olivia told me that cadaver-seeking police dogs would find Heather, maybe even helicopters because they can sense body heat.

"If you were Heather, would you want to come back after all this?" I said.

"Of course I would. Don't be dumb," she said. "They'll find her."

Hea-ther!

Poor Mr. Ollie would have a cow when he saw the Xs spray painted over his junk.

After Chicken Hill, there was more chicken to eat. And then everybody hiked to the outskirts of Fort Drum, deep in the marsh that skirted the St. Johns River. The swamp cabbage grew in thick, bushy rows and the cypresses became denser the further we trudged through the green watered marsh. I half expected to find Kidnapped Heather's skull; something crazy, her head shaved, eyes rolled to the back of her head, blood all around, teeth knocked out. I'd get the money and be Trudy's golden boy again.

We called her name over and over again. Dolores called her name the loudest.

A road sign read, *Lights On For Safety.*

Macon eventually caught up with me. His hands were filthy and his nose and neck creases were sunburned. He wore a new t-shirt under his orange vest. It had Heather Studebaker's school picture on the front. *Have You Seen Me?*

"You smell like donkey ass," I said.

"Yo, I got something to tell you but don't tell the others."

Half of the volunteers had already given up. Somebody had a heat stroke back on the footpath in the cattails. Cricket, on the other hand, didn't tire easily. She was having the time of her life counting red-winged blackbirds and collecting lucky rocks to give Kidnapped Heather when she found her.

"I know where her body is," Macon said.

"Fuck off."

"No, man. I'm serious. I know where Kidnapped Heather's body is and I'm gonna find her and prove it. If you're nice to me, we can share the money."

I pointed the Jesse James cap gun to Macon's forehead. "Where?"

He pushed my arm away. "You just gotta trust me. I'll take you to where she is when the search party's over."

I didn't believe Macon and Macon didn't believe that I believed him either.

The piggies in their cruisers accompanied what was left of the Yeehaw Junction group to the Fort Drum Service Plaza, where Kidnapped Heather had gone missing five days ago. News reporters flooded the plaza and lookie-lous came with handmade signs. Trudy said they had too many people caring about this girl.

Isn't that funny, that a person can be almost anywhere? Eventually, we'd run out of places to look. Not just in Osceola County but throughout Florida. Georgia. 'Bama, too, and everywhere else.

The candlelight vigil started at sundown.

The volunteers from Our Children Forever passed out one-wick candles. A waxy nub formed on mine. I liked the heat. I liked looking into the faces of the scared, grieving parents and old people. Lots of kids cried; mostly the girls. The boys gazed at their shoes and cracked jokes when the girls weren't looking. You'd think Kidnapped Heather had already been pronounced dead. Rafts of flowers and Beanie Babies and dollar store teddy bears and stuffed flamingos from the zoo adorned the makeshift Hope 4 Heather memorial. Teenagers made out, too. The lighting was sort of romantic. There was snickering and more heat stroke. People bowed their heads in shame because they hadn't found her yet.

Dolores Studebaker approached the podium. The U. S. of A. watched her. I'd never been so close to being on T.V. before. It was kind of cool, with the camera crew and lighting guys. Florida thought Dolores had murdered Heather. Well, maybe she did.

"My name is Dolores Studebaker and I'm a single mother from Kissimmee, Florida. My beautiful daughter Heather went missing five days ago. I'm asking for your help. Your prayers. Your bounty. Your faith. I'm asking you to help me find Heather.

"She is eleven years old. She starts seventh grade in the fall. She loves music, dancing, and sports. She's a bright, funny girl that lights up every room she's in. We must band together and do what's right. $100,000—make it $200,000, I don't care. You can have anything. You can have my life. You can have my home. Just please bring Heather back to me, safely. Please. Promise me you will help. Let's do this together. Heather, if you're watching this, please come home to me. Please know the world is looking for you."

Kidnapped Heather wouldn't be watching the news, I thought. That was dumb. She'd be watching *Johnny Bravo*. If you were really abducted, why watch something sad? People don't think.

I watched Jenna's eyes dance across the crowd of mourners. She loved misery and disaster, just like Trudy. I bet she was sorry she didn't bring the camcorder on the manhunt. She locked eyes with me, lifted her candle, and motioned for me to lift mine too. Higher than the rest of them. I did so. And then Trudy did. And everybody joined in, lifting their candles skyward and honoring Heather Studebaker with a moment of silence before "Angel" by Sarah McLachlan pulsed through the crowd on the loudspeaker. It was hard not to laugh but I played it straight. The piggies, in their costumes and badges, somberly patrolled the rows of crying people. One job to do and the piggies couldn't get it done. Not that day. Probably not tomorrow, either.

I looked over my shoulder during the song and saw Olivia standing behind me with her parents and siblings. She was sobbing her eyes out.

"I just want to find her," she squealed.

I turned back to Jenna. "Last one to find her's a rotten egg," I said, imagining a girl like Olivia murdered, with her hair matted around a tent of branches.

"We'll find her," Jenna said.

Hope 4 Heather.

Hope 4 Heather.

Hope 4 Heather.

Hope 4 Heather.

CHAPTER SIX

Osceola County Corrections Department
INTERROGATION SUBJECT: Ms. Starr Babcock
DATE: June 24, 1999, 7:32 pm
INTERVIEWED BY: Detective Linda Vallow

DETECTIVE VALLOW: Did Detective Gonzalez tell you why you're here?

STARR: Nobody said nothing to me.

DETECTIVE VALLOW: Before we dive into it, do you have something you want to tell me?

STARR: No. I don't know why I'm here. I don't know why I'm in handcuffs. I don't know why–

DETECTIVE VALLOW: You have no idea why you were arrested? Can you take a guess?

STARR: Food stamps.

DETECTIVE VALLOW: Food stamps?

STARR: Food stamp fraud. Somebody bought my stamps off me, $141 worth. I called the agency, said the neighbor stole my booklet out of the mailbox.

DETECTIVE VALLOW: No. I'm going to give it to you as straight as possible. Let's refresh your memory.

STARR: Okay, go 'head.

DETECTIVE VALLOW: Our local dispatch received a call from a plumbing technician on June 24 from 299 Northeast Sunrise Street Apt #3 in Kissimmee, Florida. The residents at that address notified the landlord, Mr. George Cruz, that there was a smell emitting from the shower every time they turned the hot water on. The landlord ignored those tenants' complaints for ten days, until the odor became so overpowering that the tenants took it upon themselves to call a plumber. A technician from Brady Brooks the Plumber Co. showed up two hours later to inspect the hot water heater and adjacent shower and toilet piping from–same address–299 Northeast Sunrise Street Apt #3. Right next to Apt #2. Are you following me?

STARR: I'm listening.

DETECTIVE VALLOW: Starr, this is where the rubber meets the road, so, I'd recommend you tell me what's going on now.

STARR: Okay. I don't know. I said I don't know. You tell me.

DETECTIVE VALLOW: Ms. Babcock, there were human body parts found in the pipes—are you following me?

STARR: Yeah, I'm with you.

DETECTIVE VALLOW: The body parts, Ms. Babcock, were in your pipes at 299 Northeast Sunrise Street Apt #2. The entry panel can only be accessed through your hallway closet: that's where all the internal plumbing is. It's a gateway to both yours and your neighbors' pipes.

STARR: You think I put them there?

DETECTIVE VALLOW: Did you?

STARR: I don't even live there anymore! Did you talk to the landlord?

DETECTIVE VALLOW: You moved? When did you move?

STARR: I live with my girlfriend. We've got a place off Dixie and Tradewinds.

DETECTIVE VALLOW: But you didn't update your address with the DMV? What about your employer? Was this a formal change-of-address? The apartment is still yours, correct?

STARR: No. We come and go. Sometimes we stay at the place I was telling you about, the Dixie and Tradewinds place, it's like a Days Inn. I don't like my apartment. I'm gonna move. I just haven't moved yet. But my stuff is there.

DETECTIVE VALLOW: Your stuff is there but you're never there?

STARR: That's right.

DETECTIVE VALLOW: So you have no idea why, when me and Detective Patti Sharp investigated your apartment—we didn't need a warrant, due to an odor of human decay all over the property by that point—at 299 Northeast Sunrise Street Apt #2 this morning—you don't know why the shower had been used just a few hours before? Hot water was still dripping out of the faucet and there was standing water in the bathtub. There was a cup of coffee in the microwave. The kitchen smelled like fresh drip coffee.

STARR: That's not mine. What did the landlord say?

DETECTIVE VALLOW: Don't worry about the landlord, Ms. Babcock. I just want to take your statement. Do you have a roommate?

STARR: Not since my ex-husband.

DETECTIVE VALLOW: When did you get divorced?

STARR: 1983.

DETECTIVE VALLOW: Where are you employed?

STARR: I was working for Gatorzone but I got suspended.

DETECTIVE VALLOW: What were you suspended for?

STARR: I was messing around after hours and stuff.

DETECTIVE VALLOW: Okay, like, trespassing?

STARR: Yeah.

DETECTIVE VALLOW: Do you have any children?

STARR: No.

DETECTIVE VALLOW: Let's return back to the scene of what I witnessed this morning. You didn't put the body parts in the pipes?

STARR: I don't know a screwdriver from a tailspin. How the fuck, ma'am, am I gonna take pipes out of a wall and stuff a body inside? That doesn't even make sense to me. That's sicko shit. Why don't you get the DNA off the pipes? Dust for my fingerprints or whatever you do.

DETECTIVE VALLOW: Any idea who the body belongs to?

STARR: Who?

DETECTIVE VALLOW: The body parts belong to an adult male, that much we know. They're at the lab now: the pipes have been uninstalled and are with forensics. Do you want to tell me who that man is, before we go through this all over again? You giving me a clear answer helps you if you are prosecuted before a trial jury.

STARR: You want me to tell you something I don't know! I don't know how he got there!

DETECTIVE VALLOW: And what about your car? Do you have something to tell me about your car?

STARR: Oh, the car. Well, that's another story.

DETECTIVE VALLOW: I'm listening. Take your time.

STARR: It smelled bad. It smelled like a dead body was in the car.

DETECTIVE VALLOW: Now we're getting somewhere. You know what? I never smelled anything so foul in my life.

STARR: Listen, I'm not a criminal, I'm not putting bodies in the plumbing or whatever. But I was afraid that the police were gonna come after me for the smell of the car. It's not what you think. I told you about the food stamps—

DETECTIVE VALLOW: You did.

STARR: I told you I worked at Gatorzone. Well, I get a call from a guy I work with that one of my baby albinos died in our manager's care. This is a baby gator, okay; small, nothing sharp about this reptile. This big—a reptile only this big. I got in trouble for trespassing after hours a couple weeks prior and was on suspension. I got pissed off when I heard about my baby, so I went back to the building at night. You'll see me on camera. I admit that. I went to the facility where there's always other workers around after hours and took the reptile home with me. I didn't tell nobody. I drove all over Orlando, Kissimmee, St. Cloud, Titusville, wherever. By the time I got back to the place I was staying at, I'd forgotten about the reptile and left it in the trunk. I forgot. I wasn't throwing some bestiality party or none of that, I forgot about it, because the guy that I was going to sell this albino gator to for his restaurant—he didn't want it anymore. I didn't have his phone number or anything. I felt obligated to bury the albino's little body, but where was I gonna do that? I didn't think it through. I decided the next day to take it to the junkyard on Chicken Hill because you don't gotta check in with nobody there. Well, the next day Gatorzone calls me back about putting me on the schedule because my probation is almost over. They gave me a choice of either part-time hours at the petting zoo land or working in the gift shop or lemonade stand. I don't like touching people's food and drinks and stuff, but that was my choice, so I went with the lemonade. I took the part-time hours. Some money is better than no money.

DETECTIVE VALLOW: Right.

STARR: So, after I got that call about going back to work, I forgot about the alligator in my trunk. So, I had the dead reptile in my car for days.

DETECTIVE VALLOW: 1989 Pontiac Firebird, correct?

STARR: I think so, yeah. I don't know cars too well.

DETECTIVE VALLOW: Okay.

STARR: Well, the next day, like I said, I went back to Gatorzone. I was parked there for six hours. After that, I drove out to Fort Drum because I was going to see my friend. And I stopped for some coffee.

DETECTIVE VALLOW: Okay. Where did you stop for the coffee?

STARR: Fort Drum Service Plaza. I was tired of being on my feet in the sun all day.

DETECTIVE VALLOW: So, you pulled to the west side of the road for a coffee, as hot as you are from standing all day in the sun. Did you do anything else while you were at Fort Drum Service Plaza?

STARR: I can't remember. I probably had to go to the bathroom and didn't want to hold it anymore. As I was in line for the coffee, I remembered the reptile in the trunk and I needed to get rid of it. I ran the hell out of there and got back in my car. I see all these people in the parking lot, shouting and going on about something. I was where the gas pumps are, sort of across. People were just gathering around. I did notice them.

DETECTIVE VALLOW: Did you stop to see what the congregating was about?

STARR: No. I figured it was a fender bender. You know how people drive out here. They drive like they've got nine lives to live. I just jumped back in my car, thinking about the animal carcass in the trunk. I realized that I could smell it. I got nervous, wondering who else can smell it and this, that, and the other. So I decided to take it out to Chicken Hill, the junkyard in Yeehaw Junction, like I told you.

DETECTIVE VALLOW: Yeehaw Junction is ten miles from Fort Drum. Why not just discard the carcass there at the rest stop?

STARR: I was scared. I didn't want anybody to see me. I wanted to get far away. I sped the whole way. Well, I get there and the gate's open.

DETECTIVE VALLOW: Did a guard or a property manager stop you, ask you where you were going?

STARR: No. I don't think nobody was around. They don't do that there, not at Chicken Hill. By now the whole car stinks and I'm just looking for a place to dump the gator. Get rid of it. I decided to dump it and go. I was suffocating from the smell at that point, and I got out of the car and heaved the little dead gator across a storage pod. I'm sure rats got to it. Or it melted in the sun. My car smelled worse the next day, even after I got rid of the animal.

DETECTIVE VALLOW: Somebody from the lab investigated your vehicle this afternoon.

STARR: Okay.

DETECTIVE VALLOW: There's evidence of human remains in your trunk.

STARR: Not human. Can't be.

DETECTIVE VALLOW: Are you sure?

STARR: I'm sure.

DETECTIVE VALLOW: Let's circle back to when you went from Gatorzone to Fort Drum Service Plaza. Do you remember the people congregating around the parking lot? A young girl went missing from that same row you were parked around the same time—the time stamp on the surveillance footage confirms that. Heather Studebaker. You've probably seen her face all over the T.V. Can you tell us anything about her?

STARR: I don't know anything.

DETECTIVE VALLOW: Ms. Babcock, where is Heather?

STARR: I don't know.

CHAPTER SEVEN

June 22, 1999. We dreamed of money and earning our keep.

We looked for the missing girl in the waste bins at Stickey's and sneaked into the rooms at Desert Inn when the maid left the door open to clean. We watched the news to see if some other lucky bastard found her in a hollow ditch. We decided which of us was guilty of abduction and where we'd be dumb enough to leave the body.

But that dirty rotten girl was still missing on June 22, 1999.

The five of us—me, Cricket, Jenna, Bam Bam, and Macon—filled canteens with rainwater in the ravine by the same grass we pissed in. We searched down in the thickets surrounding the turnpike exit ramp and listened to Eminem on the portable radio, singing about raping and killing his wife. I pulled the camo shorts down my hips so low my pubes poked out like weeds. Kidnapped Heather wouldn't know what hit her if she could hear this Eminem song, wherever the hell she was. Maybe she got dumped in the lake, too. I sang into my fist, drummed a sharp stick on a biochemical soil jar, and made all kinds of racket. The sun blazed over us. I could feel my sunburns getting sunburns. Tomorrow I'd blister.

Cricket and Bam Bam waved and shouted at the oncoming traffic as our poor, rusted down wagon still gave way to one side without its fourth wheel. We brought a pink baby carriage with us and lots of garbage bags filled with clothes we stole from the Goodwill donation bin in the Winn-Dixie parking lot. The plan was to pretend to stagger over the median and heave clothes filled trash bags into the road as oncoming vehicles got off the exit. Make it look like dead bodies everywhere. The baby carriage was an extra touch. Pretending to carry a swaddled bundle of joy would get people riled up. Jenna would catch everything on camera and sell the footage later.

Jenna sat beneath a canopy of mossy swamp cabbage in a D.A.R.E. To Keep Kids off Drugs t-shirt. She had a black eye that I suspected Ziggy gave to her, but you could never get a straight answer from Jenna. She messed with the camcorder's interior panel. The camera belonged to Ziggy and his old man. They let her use it to record dirty rotten footage. The thing was ancient, Ziggy liked to say, like 1989 ancient. But the VHS tape in the slot could be recorded over and copied. Jenna had used the same one for years now. The grainy quality meant automatic blurring out of people's faces. Jenna shouted at us from the shade to get ready, she was gonna start recording any minute.

Me and Macon had work to do. We pushed the pink baby carriage up the ramp on the shoulder of the turnpike exit. It should have gone off without a hitch.

But then everything rotten that could happen, happened.

I let go of the pink baby carriage. There was a cacophony of squealing brakes, breaking glass, and horns. Smoke flumed. An orange ring of fire exploded out from somewhere in my left periphery. My body dropped like a wet noodle and my throat burned as I crawled away, my knees scraping the blacktop.

A dude on a motorcycle rolled off his bike and onto the blacktop, too. He was on his feet in a moment, chasing after us faster than we could run. His sunglasses dangled off his ear. People screamed in vehicles behind us. Horns blared. I got the fuck up, fell down again, felt the motorcycle man's meaty hands on my ankles as I slipped out of his sweaty grasp and ran into the low-grown palmettos. I cursed, spit, then rolled away and started running up the broken fence with Bam Bam. To our left, Jenna was down in the thickets filming and Cricket, poor Cricket, crouched about twenty five feet away with our wagon, her fingers in her ears at the noise blasting, shaking like a leaf.

Blood came outta me from somewhere. It was either dripping out of my ears or my forehead, maybe my nose. But I was safe—I got away.

Macon was the slowest. He was dead meat.

We watched from the fence as the motorcycle man beat the shit out of Macon. He pummeled Macon's body into the blacktop, fists pounding his ruddy face. He jabbed punches into Macon's fat gut. The hits were almost as loud as the horns and the screaming and the sound of car alarms. The motorcycle dude body-slammed Macon again into the blacktop and blood dripped out of his head. We could see the red mix with Macon's forehead sweat, all glistening in the June sun.

"Leave him alone or I'll pop you full of lead!" I wailed, pointing the Jesse James cap gun through the chain link fence. "I'll fucking kill you! You hear me!"

When the sirens rang in the distance, the motorcycle man lifted his knee off Macon's hip and spit a loogie in his face. He returned to his bike, which was flipped over on its side, and surrounded by smoke. Cars were turned over too. I saw somebody crawl from out of their windshield, covered in broken glass.

"Come on, motherfucker! We gotta go!" I hollered at Macon.

Jenna never moved a muscle. She'd had this shit all planned out, it seemed. Capture as much footage as possible. She crouched behind a turned-over car like a gargoyle with a video camera. Nobody noticed her in the chaos anyway.

"What the fuck's she doing?" I said. I watched Jenna watch her own brother through the battered camcorder lens.

"Come on!" Bam Bam jumped up and down. "We gotta go!"

We watched through the fence as Jenna ran toward the pile-up and got down on her knees and filmed somebody's banged up face close-up, inverted in their vehicle. When Fire & Rescue and emergency services arrived, flying out with gurneys and oxygen, Jenna moved toward the turned-over vehicles, toward the chaos, not caring who saw her. But when the motorcycle man jumped off his bike again, she turned back and ran for cover, yelling for us to do the same.

"Run!" she screamed.

And Macon, not a total goner, pulled himself off the ground, blood and dirt in his hair, and wobbled toward us. He lowered himself into the palmettos and rock and climbed the fence with me and Bam Bam. Cricket came last.

"Go, go, go!" I said.

But I looked back, because I wasn't about to leave our broken wagon behind with all of our jars and biochemical grass. That was $20, just sitting.

"Just go!" Jenna said. "Leave it and fucking go!"

The five of us ran for our lives and when we realized there were a few people upon us that afternoon, our adrenaline turned into speed. We huffed and puffed all the way through the prairie, only stopping to catch our breaths at the electrical pylons at the edge of where Yeehaw Junction started. I couldn't hear. I couldn't hear anything, my ears felt clogged and full of heat and all I could hear was the screaming and horns and broken glass. My throat burned.

"I think we lost them," I said.

"We didn't lose anybody, Skeet, they quit chasing us," Jenna said.

Cricket. Poor Cricket. She was in crybaby hysterics. I'd never seen her lip quiver like that or drool and tears make a foam around her mouth. She was covered in more tears than Macon's face was smeared in blood. We didn't mention it on the walk home, but our wagon was gone. All of the biochemical soil jars. Our wood and wheels. There was at least a week's worth of cash in that thing by a fence at the turnpike.

"I thought you were gonna die," Bam Bam said.

"This would've never happened if your ass ran faster," I said. "I told you. You didn't listen. You never listen."

"Fuck off," Macon said.

Jenna cleared her throat, looking over her shoulder. I suspected she was making sure we weren't being followed. It was almost twilight. "I got it all on tape," she said. "Shit. This is the big one. This is money in the bank. This is big–real fucking big."

"I saw like ten cars crash!" Bam Bam said.

"No, you didn't," I said. "You didn't see nothing. The camera saw."

"But–"

"*Nothing*," I said.

But really, I wasn't sure. I wasn't sure what else happened out there, with the fire and all. People were dumb. If they were dumb enough to think a baby carriage sliding off a median on a highway ramp was real, they were dumb enough not to catch us once they were done piling into the ambulances and crying about it on the seven o' clock news. Stupid fucks. I reveled in watching communities cry over loss and this conundrum would be no different. On the walk home, I thought about earlier this year in April when the Columbine High School massacre happened. Dumbasses were still trying to figure that out, too. *How could this happen?* It happens the way Marilyn Manson's number one aspiring school shooter wants it to, a shirtless kid pushing a baby carriage into oncoming traffic, that's how.

When we got home to Yeehaw, it was almost dark. Trudy had a cow when she realized we didn't have the wagon with us.

"I'll send Ollie for it tonight," she said.

"You can't," Jenna said. "The highway is crawling with piggies and ambulances. It was either the wagon or six feet under for me and Macon."

"I swear on my right hook, if they find out who it belonged to–"

"Why don't you just trust me, for once?" Jenna snapped. "The wagon could belong to a bag lady or to the fucking Pope! Nobody knows shit!"

We watched the chickens cross the road. We grilled catfish and trout we caught from the stream in the ditch, smacking the fishes' heads on the plywood if they weren't all the way dead yet. We had mangos and stolen pralines for dessert. We always got our pralines from an old woman that sold out of her pick-up near Mr. Ollie's farm store.

Cricket was still shaken up. Her mood was so fouled she didn't join us in the inflatable swimming pool to take a load off. Bam Bam climbed the oak tree in the Monica Lewinsky face mask. Thunderheads came but we didn't get out of the water, even when the rain sheeted down and mosquitos sucked us dry.

"I think my tooth's gone. I swallowed it," Macon said, feeling for the space in his nasty mouth. We'd all eaten in the pool, paper plates in the grass. "That guy popped my tooth out of my jaw."

"Good," Trudy said. "You were gonna lose it 'cuz it was decaying anyway."

Later that night, me and Trudy were the only ones awake. We lay together on her mattress, watching the ceiling fan blades whip in circles as the rain hit the house. We shared a joint, clipping the ashes over the side of the bed.

"When I was a little girl," Trudy started. "You couldn't tell if it was day or night because mosquitos covered the window screens. There were so many of them stuck to the glass, so many wings, that it just looked night all the time. It looks like that tonight."

"Shit," I said. "That's too many mosquitoes."

"It was always dark," Trudy said, her rat's nest hair falling on her shoulders. She looked at me. "You hear that? You know what happens when the buzzards come?"

"What?"

"It means somebody's dead."

I nodded, exhaling a long, smoky hit.

Trudy said, "I went looking, Skeet, last night. To see who died—to see who died out in that there prairie. Because I had a bad feeling about that missing girl. So I went looking to see if it was her out there, making the buzzards with their black heads fly low, lower every time I looked."

"Then what?"

Trudy lowered her voice, just above a whisper. "I think somebody murdered that little girl and she's around here. Magpies, buzzards, it's like something out of a movie."

"Who do you think killed her?" I handed her the joint and she toked before handing it back.

"Her mama or daddy did it. It's always who's supposed to love you the most that kills you in cold blood. Hey, it's fixing to rain some more. Why don't you get some shuteye?"

But shuteye came slower than the rain did, the aluminum foil over the windows crinkling above the AC unit. Everybody else was still asleep. Lights off. Macon hadn't come to bed. I shimmied out of the house, barefoot, onto the porch and down the steps into the muddied grass.

A piggy cruiser drove by.

The wasps buzzed.

Macon was still hanging out in the inflatable swimming pool. His arms dangled over the plastic blue sides. He was up to his neck, body sunken below the surface of the rainwater-filled pool.

"Macon," I whispered.

The wasps and katydids buzzed and flew into the lights on the neighbor's double-wide. Rain hit the tin trash cans and the oak tree's silhouette loomed over Macon and the water. I called his name again. I called him a third and fourth time, too, and he still didn't respond. He didn't even twitch.

I tried one more time. "Macon?"

I put one foot in the lukewarm rainwater, splashing him over his stupid, flappy ass-body. I shoved him in the leg and finally, I shook him. His head lolled forward and he slumped to one side, his face making bubbles under the pool's surface.

Macon was dead as a doornail. I'd seen dead bodies before, lots of times, but not a snot-nosed kid, not one of us. Wings from dead bugs floated on the fabric of his trunks. His skin was tinged with shades of blue. I knelt down in the crabgrass and sniffed him, expecting decay. Nothing. I picked up Bam Bam's ceiling fan blade and poked him in the ribs. His body slumped forward, the water lapping from all sides.

I gazed over the street we lived on. At the houses and double-wides. The cars parked in the street or on lawns. The leaves on the branches. It was pitch black, but I knew where everything was. I could see past the dark.

The porch light came on. Jenna came out of the house first, smoking a cigarette, and everybody else followed suit. We surrounded the pool, looking down at Macon in the water. Trudy cursed, not wanting to deal with this nonsense. She made a phone call to Mr. Ollie, and Jenna, always our leader, told us exactly what we were going to do and how fast we had to do it. It was work time. There was no time to think and anyway I didn't really want to do much thinking right now.

And in the dark, two hours later, all of us carried Macon out to Chicken Hill to bury him.

We collectively decided it had been a head injury or internal bleeding from the beating that did him in. Maybe a combination of the two. The five of us carried him, this dead almost-a-man rocking softly between us.

A corpse is heavier dead than when he is alive. Macon's stomach gurgled when we hoisted him out of the water. Trudy carried him from the front with Macon's arms buckled under hers, and Cricket and Jenna had his legs. Me and Bam Bam did the rest, holding Macon's flabby, loaf ass above our heads.

I barfed as soon as we crossed the road into the prairie, feeling the weight of the cloudy night looming over me like a witch. Cricket suggested that perhaps Macon was in a deep sleep and would wake up tomorrow.

"Keep moving," was all Jenna said. Truth is, all of us hauling this body were like this: cold, calculated, rotten. We weren't siblings. We weren't even friends.

"Keep going. Don't stop," Trudy said, breathlessly. The back of her neck was slicked with sweat and her voice was thick. Trudy was crying. She cried like Cricket cried when she heard the motorcycle man going after Macon. He got the beating of his life.

We moved without fussing through the dark. Lovebugs zoomed around our arms and legs, our bare feet. Nothing we could do but go on. We didn't so much as crunch a single leaf or branch under our footfalls the rest of the way. The only trace was the occasional splash of water between our toes.

Macon was dead. He was really dead. Nobody out here in the world cared. Yeehaw Junction don't care. The cows don't care. The chickens don't care. The roosters don't care. The snakes don't care. The iguanas don't care. The cats don't care. Marilyn Manson don't care. Dead prostitute ghosts don't care. The motorcycle man don't care. Our Children Forever don't care. Nothing ever really happens for a reason. It's just bad every minute until it gets worse, until you're a headcase.

We walked until we couldn't see our street on the horizon line, past the red barn, past the pine tree. Mr. Ollie was waiting for us with a wheelbarrow loaded with shovels, flashlights and a pitcher of water. We dropped Macon in the grass beside his own gravesite. His arms were twisted behind his back, in a position that suggested he was ashamed of being dead. Bam Bam shined the flashlight in his eyes. They were cold, nothingness, no place normal. Trudy told Bam Bam to turn the flashlight off. Somebody could see us. And we couldn't let anybody see us.

We worked wildly, digging and shoveling, the cancer soil dusting back up into our faces like pollen, sod flying, cottontails killed, mud. My arms got so heavy I couldn't feel them anymore. I couldn't tell if I was sweating or crying. I told myself boys don't cry as mosquitoes ate me alive. *Get it together, you got a body to bury, boy.*

We dug for hours. When the trench was deep enough, we flopped Macon's body down into it, down into the dark. For a minute, I thought his face grinned up at me, but it was just the mean moonlight. A snake was slithering through the black eye sockets of somebody else's skull.

When it was over, we walked back home in the dark and didn't sleep.

At 8:49 a.m., flashing red lights danced across the Florida-room ceiling. Voices outside. Cricket clutched her gun and the kazoo. I stayed in the trash pile on the loveseat, not moving a muscle. Only my eyes darted around the room.

"Jenna?" I whispered. "Trudy?"

Cricket shushed me. "They'll hear you."

"Who?"

Then it became clear and as the sunlight seeped through the tin foil on the windows, a crawling heat up my back, I turned and watched.

"You have the right to remain silent—"

Jenna was outside our pigpen with Trudy, surrounded by piggies. Then Trudy was handcuffed, getting stuffed into the back of the cruiser.

CHAPTER EIGHT

State of Florida

HOSPITAL REPORT OF DEATH (PAGE 1 OF 2)

OSCEOLA COUNTY HOSPITAL

D.O.A. JUNE 29, 1999

PATIENT DATA

Boyd, Stuart, W.

SSN 999-19-6606

1112 W. Mountain Way, Seattle, Washington, 98116

RELIGION: Unknown

TIME OF DEATH: approx 2:00 a.m. June 29, 1999

TREATMENT ADMINISTERED: N/A

MEDICAL EXAMINER PRESENT: Yes

CAUSE OF DEATH (or as a consequence of): Homicide

APPROX INTERVAL BETWEEN ONSET & DEATH (1): Unknown, under investigation

ANTECEDENT CAUSES (2):

>21 stab wounds to the back, torso, left arm

>Blunt-force to the extremities

>Missing (6) fingers

>Missing right arm/hand extremities

>Missing approx. 1.5 of right thigh to right ankle

OTHER SIGNIFICANT CONDITIONS CONTRIBUTING TO DEATH (3): Sepsis, severe dehydration

HOSPITAL REPORT OF DEATH (PAGE 2 OF 2)
OSCEOLA COUNTY HOSPITAL
D.O.A. JUNE 29, 1999

PATIENT DATA

>Boyd, Mallory, K.

>SSN 321-12-3213

>1112 W. Mountain Way, Seattle, Washington, 98116

>PREGNANT AT TIME OF DEATH: Yes

>RELIGION: Unknown

>TIME OF DEATH: approx 2:00 AM, June 29, 1999

>TREATMENT ADMINISTERED: N/A

>MEDICAL EXAMINER PRESENT: Yes

CAUSE OF DEATH (or as a consequence of): Homicide

MATERNAL DEATH: approx. 32 weeks pregnant

APPROX INTERVAL BETWEEN ONSET & DEATH (1): Unknown, under investigation

ANTECEDENT CAUSES (2):

> 14 stab wounds to the cranium, neck, torso
>
> Missing (1) fetus

Umbilical stump mostly intact, 2" of umbilicus anchored to vaginal wall. Amniotic sac punctured by same weapon used to remove fetus: kitchen shears concealed behind placenta (intact). Uterine cavity retains normal prenatal characteristics, lining of blood, tissue, etc.

OTHER SIGNIFICANT CONDITIONS CONTRIBUTING TO DEATH (3): Sepsis, dehydration

CHAPTER NINE

JUNE 23, 1999. Black-winged moths fluttered in the lamp light above the mattress. Rain drummed the windows as I tossed restlessly. Again and again, I dreamt about dumping Macon's body into the hole. When I closed my eyes, I could hear his neck snap. Wagon's gone, Macon's gone, Trudy's gone, all in a flash, like the bloodsucking larvae that once swarmed Trudy's bedroom window.

"Skeet," Cricket whispered, next to me. "I can feel the baby kicking."

My eyes shot open. "That's swell," I said.

Cricket had cried so much over Macon that her crow's feet got a rash. Her dimples were swollen pink. She sat up on her elbows, looking at me next to her on the mattress. We slept with a single bed sheet in the summer. Too hot for much else.

"I think I know the name of the baby now."

"You do?"

"Lil Trudy." She flipped onto her side, rubbing her belly in circles. "When's Trudy coming home, Skeet?"

"I dunno."

"Can you please find out?"

But what happened after that was we fell back asleep for hours, not rousing until it was almost dark again. Bam Bam, too. Never even got out of bed to piss. When it started pouring rain and the screen door in the Florida-room wiggled in the stormy breeze, I dragged myself out of bed to find Jenna and Ziggy counting cash. I wasn't so good with numbers, but there was a lot of dough spread out in front of them.

Jenna hadn't slept. She looked wired, wide-eyed like maybe she was drinking too much RC Cola. Ziggy's greasy ponytail stuck up all over. *Married ... With Children* played on mute on the T.V.

"What do you want?" Jenna said, not looking up. "Nyquil's in the fridge. Back to bed."

"But I'm awake."

"Let him stay," said Ziggy, shooting me a look.

I paced down the hallway, slipped into the kitchen, walked out to the porch, thought about having a cigarette until something to say popped into my head. I returned to the living room. "Is that bail to get Trudy out of the slammer?"

"Mind your business," Jenna said.

I paid no mind to the cash, crushing empty soda bottles under my ass as I wriggled into the shopping cart. I fished the clicker out of the clothes and put on the news to see Kidnapped Heather's school picture flashing again on the screen.

...still at large. Day 8 in the Hope 4 Heather case in Central Florida. A man was arrested this afternoon in Apopka on probable cause that authorities are keeping hush for now. More information when we have it.

There was a segment about Hope 4 Heather where the reporter asked townies at a Publix deli counter in Kissimmee what they thought should happen next in the case, what with her fliers and pictures all over the fucking state. Everybody thought her mama might have done it and that segment alone lulled me into another coma. I didn't awake for another hour when a Monica Lewinsky-masked Bam Bam, and Cricket, wearing Macon's oversized No Fear t-shirt, stood over me. Jenna and Ziggy seemed long gone. So was the cash. Cricket asked me if I could hear Macon's voice.

"Hear him?" I repeated.

"I think I heard him crying," said Bam Bam through Monica Lewinsky's mouth. He stuck a finger in my ear and I swatted his gross paws away. "It woke me."

Cricket said, "Me too. We think he might still be alive out there."

"But you can't come back to life."

Cricket considered this, rubbing her belly in circles. She took a deep breath. "I think we made a humongous mistake. Listen! Listen and you can hear him!"

I hated Macon with every bone in my body. But I wasn't the one that had been beaten to a pulp and died in the inflatable swimming pool on a rainy summer night. There was something in the air, though—a voice, a whimper, light as coins clinking in a clutch purse.

"Shoot," I said. "If he's still alive we could get in big trouble. I'm not going to no boys' prison."

Cricket blew the kazoo. She frowned, slipping it back in her jean shorts pocket. "Do you want to know what I think? I think they arrested Trudy because they caught us burying Macon. So, if he's not really gone, we can go get him and show the piggies and bring Trudy back. It's a mis-*understanding*."

"Get your gun, girl. We have to unbury him."

Cricket rubbed her belly. "Look at my fingernails how much dirt there is. It's not good for the baby inside me."

The three of us hiked to Mr. Ollie's property side by side, picking up the pace. My calves ached from carrying a dead man the night before. I wore my orange rescue vest. We couldn't remember the marker where we buried him–did we bury him before the barn, or after?

The trek back to Macon's grave was wet from our sweat and muggy from the rain, overcast with smelly magpies flying as low as Trudy said they would. It was so quiet except for the occasional truck in the distance. I could hear the cows chomping in the grass near the red barn. First thing I'd do when we unburied Macon was kick him in the dick for tricking us and for making me cry like a pussy pants. But we didn't make it to Macon's grave because something caught our attention a mile into our journey.

I silenced Cricket and Bam Bam Lewinsky with the magic finger. I parted the canopy of palmettos, our feet clearing the path. Gnats scattered. There was a forest green Ford Explorer sticking out of the sinkhole. Its Explorer ass up in the air, rear tires off the ground, the engine cut but ticking away. A white woman crawled out of the backseat window, looking as scatterbrained as the curly towhead pulling himself out of the trenches beside her. They didn't see us. Not yet. I caught what they were saying—some cursing, what-happened, are-you-okay, the usual suspects. They had clean hair and paddle boards strapped to the roof of the car. They surveyed their mess in the sinkhole, regaining some bearings–if they ever had any to begin with. The black, crumbly hole before us had to be some 12 ft x 12 ft, and dirt still plunged over the vehicle.

"Here, piggy, piggy," Bam Bam said. "Oinkers at five o' clock."

Me and Cricket locked eyes. I steadied my grip on the Jesse James cap gun and walked toward the two travelers, who were clearly piggies undercover. They were too near Macon's grave, too cleaned up, to be anything but piggies.

"Hey, mister," I said. "Nice pit. What brings you to our neck of the woods? You know where you're at?"

They drew their attention to us standing there in the shadows of the tangled brambles. They were both blond, wearing earth tones and some kind of suede sandal with straps. But the woman. The woman was pregnant. Ready-to-pop-any-minute pregnant with her hands protectively over the belly. I wanted to see inside, make sure it was a real belly and not a fake one like Cricket's.

"Watch your step, there's a sinkhole. It ate my rental," Towhead said.

"You don't say," I said.

They introduced themselves as Stu and Mallory Boyd from Seattle.

"Never heard of it," said Cricket.

"So much for the scenic route," Stu bellowed, taking a second look at the four-and-a-half-foot tall boy in a Lewinsky mask. "We were headed for Interstate 95. Thought we'd see some farm country beforehand. Before we knew it–"

"Thickets get thick," I said. "Nobody comes this way. It's private property."

Stu gazed at his old lady, asking her if she was hurt. He asked about the baby. How did she feel. I flashed my mossy teeth at them.

"We're in a bind," Mallory explained. "This is a rental. I need to call our AAA immediately. Nearest phone? Gosh, there wasn't even a warning sign."

"Say," Cricket said, poking at her own belly. "You're gonna be a mama like me. I'm expecting, too! This is really special meeting like this. At two months, the fetus is developing its face and limbs. And for $2, you can use our phone back at our little house up the road. And two pregnant mamas–me and you!"

Mallory smiled feebly.

Stu scratched his head, waving away the gnats. "You'd think your councilman would do something about the sinkhole."

"You'd think," I said, not moving a muscle.

Fearfulness seeped into Mallory's eyes when me and Cricket circled the mass pit, and then the two of them, with their ugly sandals in the dirt. Hypothetical thumbs up their assholes. Mallory crossed her arms over her belly and didn't let go. She demanded to know which way to a phone and if the barn belonged to us or our "parents."

"Drugstore," Mallory said. "What about a drugstore? Do you have those out here?"

"I see Southern hospitality thrives on the Florida panhandle this millennium. Come on, Mallory. We're not staying here," said Stu. "I'll handle this."

But Stu Boyd from Seattle couldn't handle it because Stu Boyd's head spun when Cricket lifted the .22 handgun out of her jean shorts and gripped it like Will Smith in *Independence Day*, only without the quips and alien moon landing. I followed suit with the Jesse James cap gun. Bam Bam used finger guns.

Mallory cried out.

"Oink oink," said Bam Bam. His voice was muffled by Monica Lewinsky.

"You got a badge?" said Cricket.

"You're on thin ice," I said.

"Whoa, whoa." Stu put his hands up like he was in a movie and surrendering. "We're not cops. We don't have badges, guys. We're tourists. We thought taking some of the backroads would be a fun way to explore all that Florida has to offer-"

I hocked a loogie into the grass. "Yeehaw Junction don't got nothing to offer," I said. "You took Trudy away on our own turf."

"Stu-" Mallory whined.

"We don't want trouble," Stu said. "Trust me in that."

"I ain't big on trust, is what," I said.

"We have business out here," said Cricket. Her face relaxed, approaching Mallory with the gentleness of a housecat. "Your hair. It's so *pretty*. It reminds me of Trudy's hair. Is it so pretty because of your prenatal vitamins?"

"Don't touch me, please!" said Mallory, hands splayed over her belly. "I do not consent!"

"You hear that?" I said. "She doesn't want to be touched."

"But I like her hair!"

"Not now, Cricket," I said. "Why don't y'all come on back to the little house up the road with us and you can use our phone to call your rental place."

"We have cash," said Stu. "I'm going to reach into my back pocket and retrieve my wallet."

"Do you know why they call it Jackass Crossing? Because you'd have to be a jackass to get stuck in our sinkhole." Cricket giggled.

"Oink oink," Bam Bam said again.

I swallowed the lump in my throat. "Law's laid out. You piggies hand us your wallets and come back with us. You run, we shoot you and the bun in your oven. We bring you back with us anyway. Don't draw attention or I'll shoot you."

Stu lifted a finger into the air. "Son—"

"I'm nobody's son. Now back to our house before I make you, piggy, into bacon."

"Please. Don't do this. We're just tourists!" Mallory whimpered. "We're driving to the Keys!"

"Keys ain't much better than here," I said, raising the Jesse James cap gun. "March. Let's go."

It was obvious that Stu and Mallory Boyd from Seattle had never had guns pointed at them before. Not even finger guns. They seemed to think there were more of us hidden in the tall prairie grass, waiting to clobber them. And although Stu and Mallory wailed in terror and said a prayer under their breaths, and told each other it was going to be okay, they begged us only once to let them go, and didn't run. For one thing, Mallory waddled like a drunk duck. She couldn't go fast and her breathing was labored, huffing and puffing all over the place. It was funny to watch. Exciting, too.

It was like I was holding three people hostage and not just two. Her and Stu's hands never left that big belly.

We hiked back and crossed the road without a hitch. Mallory gazed at me miserably, then tripped on the bottom porch step of the old white house. In retaliation, I screamed at her for fucking it up, demanding she get inside.

"Look where you're stepping," I said. "Don't scuff the scuff marks. We don't rape but we shoot. We're not gonna stick you with anything. We kill rapists with gunfire, don't we, Cricket?"

"But not my daddy. We don't kill my daddy," Cricket replied from behind me, scrambling into the house.

"Right, Cricket. Everybody except your daddy."

I kicked Mallory behind her knee and she shot into the Florida-room screen, hollering like the sow she was. She tried grabbing a broom to defend her pathetic piggie self, but she was too fat and missed as I kicked the broom out of her direction. She slammed her head on the wood floor and whinnied. It was the funniest sound I'd ever heard in your life.

Hell broke loose inside the old house.

Stu took a swing at Cricket's face. I hit him hard in the kidney with my knuckles out like Trudy taught me. I kept striking him until Bam Bam, sharp as hell, stabbed Stu in the shin with a pitchfork he grabbed from the shopping cart. The pitchfork clanged to the wooden floor but Bam Bam picked it up again and got Stu in his meaty back. Blood pooled in the man's shirt. Mallory stumbled like bumped-over roadkill. Her hands swam wildly in the air, desperate for balance.

Hearing the fight, Jenna dashed out of the bedroom and into Mallory, grabbing her by the hands and yanking her forward, a cracking, whistle sound coming from Mallory's biceps. Mallory cried out in terror.

"I got her!" Jenna said. Her eyes flashed. "Who the fuck is this?"

Next door, the dog barked at our commotion.

"Undercover pigs. Sinkhole. Watching us," I said, catching my breath.

Mallory begged Jenna to stop as she straddled her. Jenna grabbed a blow dryer from the trash-filled tub and hit Mallory in the head with it, so Mallory quit the crying bit. Jenna yelled for Bam Bam to get the video camera—it was on the loveseat. Still shirtless and now peppered in Stu's blood, Bam Bam snatched the bulky camcorder and tossed it to Jenna. The planks underneath our feet creaked. I felt like we were going to bust right on through them.

Cricket stuck the .22 handgun against Stu's neck and the two of us dragged him into the bathroom. I pushed him into the bathtub with the trash and filthy linens. The weight of his legs kicked the toilet paper rolls into the air. He was half conscious, screaming for me to stop. Cricket grabbed a leftover biochemical soil jar and shook it frantically in Stu's face as her other hand gripped the gun. Jenna dragged Mallory into the bathroom by clutching a fistful of her straight blond hair. I got crushed against the door, wiggling out between them as Mallory got pushed into the bathtub with her towhead beau.

"Two dollars! Two dollars!" Cricket leaned over the open toilet bowl like it was an armchair until she could reach the bathtub. She clasped a handful of Mallory's hair and breathed it in. "It smells so pretty!"

Jenna clicked open the camcorder's panel and began filming everything from the doorway.

Mallory pleaded for their baby's life, nonsensically hysterical. She cried that she was 33 weeks pregnant and to please, oh, please don't hurt the baby. It was hard to understand her over the cry baby stuff.

"Please," Stu said, opening one eye. "Leave her alone."

Boys don't cry, I realized. Men do. And this man was no boy, no rottweiler-little-man if I'd ever seen one. I thought about killing and the sweet release that would boil through me if I killed. It would feel like nothing else on this earth, killing would. And I was man enough to do it.

I screamed bloody murder into Stu's face, as loud as I could, crazy eyes and spit flying. I could smell his blood. My eardrum hummed out again. I screamed and screamed and screamed against his face.

"Please," Mallory begged. "Don't do this."

The barking dog next door went wild, snarling and howling like it was fighting off an army.

Jenna positioned the camcorder on the edge of the sink.

"Piggie cunts get their cake and eat it too," I said, popping Mallory in the jaw. Hitting her hurt my fist, too, but I did it one more time for good measure anyway.

Jenna came up behind me, told Cricket to move it, and wrangled Mallory's broken arms together at the elbows to tie them together with the nylon and rope we kept under the sink for times like this.

"And don't fuck with my knots. I didn't learn it from Girl Scouts," Jenna said, hovering over Mallory as her screams echoed back at us.

Jenna taped Mallory's mouth and then Stu's too. Stu could barely get a word out. We tied Stu's hands behind his back and then forced his body down into the trash in the bathtub as it spilled all over the both of them and onto the grimy linoleum floor; his body weight, pooled in blood, crushed both of his arms.

"Oink, oink, oink, oink, oink, oink, oink!" Bam Bam pounded his fists onto the hallway wall.

I screamed in Stu's face again, just to scream, just to show him violence.

"Please," Mallory blinked, covered in her own snot from her filthy, wet nose. "God save my baby!"

Jenna picked up the camcorder and stood over the bathtub, zooming in on Mallory's violated face. Jenna smiled.

She said, "God is dead."

"God is dead, knucklehead," I said.

Cricket gently retrieved the handgun from its nice holster in her jean shorts and showed it to the young couple. She drew it close to their faces. Mallory's breathing picked up.

"It's not even loaded," Cricket laughed. "Silly dillies. I haven't taken my gun lessons yet. Mr. Ollie says I have to earn my bullets but we've been looking for Kidnapped Heather so I haven't gotten much practice."

"Put it away," Jenna said. "You're in my camera shot."

Cricket cooperated. "I love your hair, Mallory. I'd love to hold your baby, too. I can hold mine in this arm and yours in this arm like this, see?" She mimicked a rock-the-baby movement. "I wonder what color the baby's hair is."

We were thunder, out of control, primal. I was the control, the youngblood, the bastard from Yeehaw Junction I'd always wanted to be.

CHAPTER TEN

WWW.DIRTYHUMANMARKET.TOR.ONION.Z1CHAMPS
DO YOU LIKE VIOLENCE?
RAW! Shock, Gore, Snuff, VIOLENCE.
UNEDITED NO BULLSHIT.
FILMED IN FLORIDA.
USER: youngblood2001
USER SINCE: November 1997
LAST ONLINE: June 1999

First 10 seconds of all videos are FREE - PREVIEW HERE
$5 for ONE RAW VIDEO CLIP
$30 FOR A 2-HOUR RAW VHS
$40 FOR ALL CLOTHING ITEMS

Transfers to VHS ONLY. Add $5 to mail.
Pick-up is FREE at Gatorzone parking lot in Orlando, FL.
No exceptions!!!!!!!!!!

Browse Video Categories by user youngblood2001

Lightning Strikes

Man struck by train tracks 00:02:13

Vestibule trauma center man after lightning

strike - CONTORTED BODY! 00:03:14

Toddler lightning strike by swimming pool 00:01:45

Man lightning strike DEAD INSTANTLY 00:01:01

Lightning strike in Ocala Nation-

al Forest CRAZY STORM 00:04:35

Homeless guy hit by lightning side of building 00:03:10

Lightning day after hurricane (Free with any

purchase, but ASK me to include it) 00:02:25

9-1-1 Call Transcript Old Lady and

Operator lightning strike 00:05:50

9-1-1 Call Transcript Homeless guys 00:01:41

Lightning strike in yeehaw junc-

tion by Desert Inn BOOM! 00:04:19

Middle School Fights

Hair ripped out 00:08:20

2 boys, 3 girls BLOOD EVERYWHERE

IN GYM GANG FIGHT 00:06:25

2 girls punching and kicking COPS CALLED 00:11:09

CRAZY ASS OUT FIGHT

READING CLASSROOM 00:05:01

Cafeteria fight jun food line 00:02:13

Cafeteria fight #2 00:00:45

Cafeteria fight #3 00:01:25

Cafeteria fight COPS CALLED 00:08:01

Cafeteria food fight 00:02:48

CRAZY CAFETERIA FOOD FIGHT
WWJD? KIDS FIGHTING 00:06:36
FACULTY AND KIDS GANG FIGHT 00:01:05
Cafeteria food fight 00:08:30
Gang fight on sidewalk 00:05:00
Security guard Mr. Thomas check-
ing out Gurlz asses 00:03:00
Knife fight after bomb threat WALK OUT!!!! 00:09:37
Knife fight in Girls Bathroom 00:06:42
Knife fight in girls restroom 00:02:37
Basketball court FIGHT WITH BLOOD 00:10:01

High School Fights
Girl beats up cafeteria lady 00:01:02
Cafeteria prank TEACHER FALLS
AND BLACKS OUT 00:04:30
Security guard shot by student in portable! 00:07:03
2 girls FIGHT IN LOCKER ROOM! 00:11:17
Girls fight football field 00:04:30
Cafeteria fight 00:02:19
CRAZY FIGHT TEETH KNOCKOUT IN GYM!!! 00:07:59
2 boys KNIFE FIGHT POLICE CALLED! 00:13:44
Girl MOLESTED in school bathroom 00:04:21
Cafeteria fight CRAZY CRAZY 00:09:01
Flag pole prank KID BLACKS OUT 00:07:00
Restroom prank 00:04:06
Faculty fight at baseball game 00:05:22
Kid Threatens Math Teacher 00:00:33
Fart prank on Math Teacher 00:01:03
Gurlz bathroom trash and toilets TOUR 00:09:11
Boys bathroom trash and toilets TOUR 00:04:35

VIOLENCE, GORE, SICK SHIT
Crazy Ecstasy DEATH AT SEARS!!
(from Valdosta, GA) 00:04:10
Kids faces blown off at party 00:09:59
9-1-1 call during SHOOTING AT WAFFLE
HOUSE (from Statesboro, GA) 00:01:19
Forced to PULL OUT OWN TEETH
WHILE DANCING 00:05:23
Forced to PULL OUT OWN TEETH
WHILE DANCING #2 00:04:56
TRIPPING BALLS FREAKOUT ON E 00:04:01
Some girl eats her own shit for $50 00:03:20
Stabbed to death in movie theater 00:15:00
Kurt Cobain Suicide CRIME SCENE FOOTAGE
RAW! - copies of photos $100 TOTAL
PROOF OF U.F.O. in Groom Lake,
FL - copies of photos $50 TOTAL
Extraterrestrial footage from
1955 Sugar Bends, FL - 00:14:29
Weird paranormal shit from Briggs Valley 00:04:12
CRAZY FIGHT breaks out on It's A
Small World ride at Disney!!!! 00:00:47
Guy jizzes in Wendy's frosty, then serves it!!!!! 00:02:15
Wife calls 9-1-1 on husband, then decap-
itated!!!!! (from Statesboro, GA) 00:12:12
Electrocution in plastics factory 00:03:32
Suicide in house, shoots self 00:12:02
1955 U.S. MILITARY POISONS YEEHAW
JUNCTION DDT SPRAYS 00:14:24
ORIGINAL DDT SPRAY COMMER-
CIALS IN FLORIDA 1955-1966 00:04:31
Walmart fights compilation

Service Merchandise theft compilation
(Used) menstrual period pads - Collected at high schools, train station, Gatorzone
(Used) tampons - Collected at Gatorzone, high schools, train station

CLOTHING AND DIRTY ROTTEN!!!!
Various strips of clothing from abductions age 3 - 21
Boys AND Girls
Shoes, socks, zipper jackets, hats, etc.
CLOTHING WITH BLOOD BY APPOINT
ONLY: LIMITED AVAILABILITY
Toenail clippings from dead pros-
titutes including overdoses
Fingernails from dead children
Toenails from dead children
Suicide photos DELUXE PACKAGE BY AP-
POINTMENT ONLY: LIMITED AVAILABILITY
Fingernails from suicides (blood
a possibility, but not guaranteed)
Toenails from suicides (blood not guaranteed!!!!!)
REALISTIC Monica Lewinsky mask
WITH REAL BLOOD SPLATTER
Gurlz scrunchies
Boyz tube socks
Various shoes BY APPOINTMENT
ONLY: LIMITED AVAILABILITY
Various teeth from all ages, sizes, structure, adult molars, etc.
ASK!!!! BY APPOINTMENT ONLY!!!!

CHAPTER ELEVEN

JUNE 25, 1999. I was packing heat with Cricket's Survivor Day handgun in my camo shorts and it made me feel like I had a second dick. I kept the faith: today would be the day I'd shoot up the slammer where Trudy was being held like a dairy cow. That morning, in the tangerine light, me and Cricket went to Chicken Hill with Mr. Ollie to shoot beer cans off a slope where we'd once blown up leaf blowers with sugar rockets. Cricket had a better aim than me, but boy howdy, did she flounder at the sound of the gun. And the smell of the gunpowder in the air was rancid, too.

After shooting, I had things to prove. We hitchhiked, Jenna and me. We were headed to the middle school in Kissimmee where Kidnapped Heather had attended sixth grade. (Easier to get around in the school, too, since it was a late summer session because of an active storm season or some such bologna.) I didn't want to go, but Jenna implied that we'd stop at the slammer to see Trudy. Plus, Jenna made a lot of dough off her dirty rotten regulars: the teachers at the school. Today, we were going to make a delivery to Mr. Dukakis.

Jenna and I rode in the backseat of a station wagon with a Black man blasting surf ska and his little daughter in the passenger side eating zebra cakes. There was a plastic lady in a hula skirt hanging off the rear view with her tits out. I felt like a golden retriever sniffing the skunky air as we made miles on the interstate.

Jenna hitchhiked to Kissimmee all the time to film students. She got footage of everything; from girls' nail-polished toes in flip-flops, to hallway fights, to teachers stealing computers, and, once, a miracle. A bow-legged sixteen-year-old girl stood from her wheelchair and danced for Jenna in the girls' gym bathroom. The wheelchair miracle girl took off her puka necklace and raked the white, rough, square shells through her fingers. It was wild. People loved white girl miracles especially when they involved recovered paralysis or found freedoms.

Jenna made more money on that miracle-in-a-wheelchair footage than any other. The second most popular was a video of Trudy rubbing one out while holding an urn filled with somebody's grandaddy's ashes. With Macon six feet under, I'd have to take note on how to make a buck like this. We had mouths to feed: ours. And Trudy expected us to help with the selling because she gave us a roof over our heads, which meant we were less likely to get snatched unlike Kidnapped Heather.

"Hey, girl," I said, to the little girl eating the zebra cakes. "You think the world's gonna end when 2000 comes? You think the planes will explode when midnight strikes?"

"I dunno."

"What about the computers? If the computers go, we all go."

She shrugged. "If the computers get messed up, they'll fix them."

"Who will?"

"The government people. I don't know, who cares."

Well, the little girl was right. Who cares? Let us all die at the strike of midnight. Better to die on 12/31/99 before computers and planes self-deconstructed to maim and murder. They were probably programmed to militarize piggies and kill Blacks for giving poor white trash a piggyback ride to school. Anyone who cared about people staring at them riding in a Black man's car had a brain the half-size of a racist rooster. Piggies get badges because they're too scared to blow their brains out. Maybe everybody's too birdbrained to realize that the year 2000 wasn't going to be here so we could fill up our time roaming strip malls and eating at Long John Silver's. There were more important things. Dangerous things. Everybody was nervous, even me, but I couldn't tell you why because I never cared about nothing that wasn't for me.

I wrote **$cumbag** with my wet finger on the rear window. I underlined it as the trumpet and bass blared from the car stereo.

"Say," I said, nudging Jenna next to me. "How far is the jail from the school?"

Jenna had a smudge of mascara inked across her cheekbones. Between her knees, she had a purple Eastpak stuffed with whatever she'd planned on selling, and the camcorder.

"Quit asking questions," Jenna said. "This is business, not game time."

Game time.

I picked my pockets for what was left of my cigarettes (Newports) and offered one to the girl. "Trade you a smoke for a zebra cake," I said.

The girl looked at her old man but he was singing that surf ska, riding on a wave inside of his own head. She took the cigarette furtively and handed me over the creamy cake that I ate in one big bite, gumming the chocolate cream. I used my sticky finger to circle **$cumbag** on the car window. The brown, misshapen mole on my right hand pulsed with prickling pain.

The singing dude dropped us off in front of Kissimmee Park Middle School by the bronze pelican statue, the school's mascot. The American flag flapped at half mast for Hope 4 Heather. The school was a one-level building surrounded by windowless portables, a gymnasium closed due to asbestos, a computer room, and a running track behind the cafeteria. I blended in, walking down the outdoor corridor and through the noisy hallways swollen with students. I saw a tall kid wearing a Marilyn Manson t-shirt and silver studded jewelry. He didn't know Marilyn Manson like I knew Marilyn Manson. He didn't know that Marilyn Manson was dangerous, just like me. I shot the kid a dirty look and he shot me one back.

Jenna disclosed my instructions: "When the first bell rings, that means lunch. When the second bell rings, everybody goes to class. When the third bell rings, that means it's lunch again. I'll meet you back here, in front of the Hope 4 Heather wall, at the third bell. Got it?"

"Can I get a chocolate milk?"

"Hang tight and we'll fucking see."

Jenna left me by the Hope 4 Heather memorial wall outside of the cafeteria. There were teddy bears and balloons and heart-shaped paper roses and a God Will Find You Baby banner covered in glitter and stickers of manatees, plus homemade cards with lousy handwriting and dry-inked marker. *I Miss You. Jesus Bring Her Home. Come Home Soon. We Support You at Kissimmee Park.* And one, now-famous flier: *Have You Seen Me?*

Kids bustled out of classrooms. Lockers opened and slammed. Benches grated across the vinyl floor. I'd never been around so many kids before. I didn't care for it much. I looked over my shoulder to see Olivia, the girl from the search and rescue mission, looking back at me.

"Skeet?" She wore denim overalls and a soccer jersey. "I thought it was you. You go here now?"

"Nah," I said. "I'm here on business."

"Oh." Long beat. "Are you on the safety patrol or something?"

I looked down at my orange rescue vest from the search, over the D.A.R.E. To Keep Kids off Drugs t-shirt I stole from Jenna—a little bloodied still from the day of Macon's accident.

"I'm not on nothing," I said. "You're thinking something bad about me, the way you're looking—"

"I'm not thinking anything."

"You're looking at my black eye."

"You get socked? Like, in a fight?"

I touched the tender skin around my eyebrows. Mallory, our gang's favorite tourist, who was currently bleeding and sobbing in our bathtub, got me at least twice during the brawl. "It's nothing."

Olivia moved a foot closer to me. She tucked her hair behind her ear, opening the front hardcover of an algebra textbook. "Want to see something?" She handed me a folded note. "Read it. It's from Heather the Friday before she went missing."

I unfolded it and pretended to skim it. Print was fine, but I couldn't do nothing with handwriting. "Read it for me. I don't got time to read."

"Okay," Olivia said. "It says: *Pool Party at 5 p.m. It's gonna be the bomb.*" She snatched it back and refolded it. "Yeah, we were supposed to have a pool party at my grandma's house on the last day of school. Now Heather's not here. It's weird."

I shrugged, scoffing inside at her useless tenderness.

"That's nothing. You want to see something secret?"

It just so happened that Olivia did want to see a secret. All girls did. I convinced her to come with me into the girls' bathroom, the one outside of the cafeteria. "GAY" was marked on the mirror in lipstick. We went into the wheelchair stall, closing the lock, both of our sneakers in toilet water puddles on the filthy linoleum. It smelled like piss and hairspray. Olivia folded her arms, her gaze floating down my bloody D.A.R.E. t-shirt to my torn chucks. She looked nervous. She seemed to think I was going to show her my dick.

I whispered, "Ever fired a gun before?"

Suddenly, the bathroom got noisy with girls coming and going, slamming doors, laughing, toilets flushing. We stayed in the stall and stared at each other.

"I said, 'You ever fired a gun before?'"

"No."

I could smell bubblegum on her breath but I think she swallowed it after I gave her a quiet motion with my index finger. *Shh.* I gently lifted Cricket's Survivor Day handgun out of my shorts. Olivia's blue eyes bugged out. Her lips trembled. She didn't move until she blinked.

"It's real," I whispered. "You can't hold it but you can touch it if you want to."

"I don't know—"

"Don't act like a baby," I said.

Olivia's eyes brimmed with tears.

"Go ahead," I said. "Feel it."

Her voice trembled. "Where did you get that?"

The air dryers went off.

"It doesn't matter," I said. "Just touch it."

Olivia averted her eyes from the handgun, a teardrop hitting her lip. She wiped it away.

"Why are you being a baby?" I whispered.

Olivia's hand shook as her fingertips reached for the unpolished barrel. She smoothed her fingertips over it like she was petting an iguana at the zoo.

"I got a bullet too," I said. "Want to help me load it?"

The worn tips of our shoes touched. The linoleum was squeaky underneath us as we moved closer together, holding the handgun at the same time, breathing on each other. Olivia was right there, so close to my black eye and ruddy face. It seemed only natural to kiss her but before I could get my lips on her lips, she stormed out of the bathroom stall, acting like I'd shown her my dick and balls or some shit.

"Fine. Act like that," I said. "Bitch."

I stuffed the handgun back in my shorts and whipped my fist into the stall door. I left the bathroom. I went to stand in front of the Hope 4 Heather wall and stole a chocolate milk off of a kid's lunch tray. Jenna joined me after the third bell. She had the camcorder and was interviewing seventh graders with their mouths full of wires. Brace-faces.

"So, what do you think happened to Heather?" Jenna asked one boy.

"I think she faked it. She's probably hiding in her bedroom or in a closet and her parents just don't want to tell the truth."

Jenna asked, "Can you elaborate?"

"It's just something that Heather Studebaker would do. She'd have played a trick on everybody. I think she's not even really missing. Like, her parents created this hoax to get people to care and give them charity money. She's famous."

Jenna asked another student, a kid with a backpack on wheels and gym shorts.

"What about you? What do you think happened to Heather?"

"I think she probably killed herself."

"Tell us more," said Jenna.

The kid shrugged, looking as dumb as a bag of hammers. "A lot of these missing Florida cases end up being suicides in the river. My dad works for the deputy and half of the calls are are just fuck-ups, using drugs or whatever."

Another kid, a couple inches taller than his gym-shorts wearing friend, piped up. "I think somebody in the family did it. Probably the dad. She didn't have a boyfriend."

Jenna approached a girl rummaging through her school locker. "Hey, you. What do you think happened to Heather?"

"I think we never really knew her, you know? I mean, how can they not find her? I think she's still in Florida and out there, safe, fending for herself. Maybe she's trying to find her way home."

"That's nice," said Jenna, in a tone I'd never heard her use before.

I downed two cartons of chocolate milk before stealing a third, and by that time, it was time to visit with Mr. Dukakis. He was the whole reason we were here in the first place, and I suspected Jenna was selling him a video tape or underwear out of the Eastpak.

Mr. Dukakis' room was at the end of a long hallway with classrooms on either side. Kids zipped by, clomping down the halls. Lockers shut and whistles blew. The fluorescent lights were off, the place was pretty dim, quiet. Through the narrow window, we watched Mr. Dukakis writing at his desk. He was thirty-something, close to Stu and Mallory's age. He had a double chin and a white patch of hair pushed back like a mop. There was a spiky-haired kid in the front row writing furiously on what could only be test paper. Lights were off. Me and Jenna walked in.

There was a streak of chalk powder on the board, rows of empty desks because it was lunch, and loose leaf paper sticking out of cubby holes. I sat in the back row like Zack Morris on *Saved by the Bell*, because everything I knew about school I learned from *Saved by the Bell*. Jenna sat in the first row.

Mr. Dukakis calmly got up from his desk and taped a sheet of yellow construction paper to the window in the door, so only a shaft of light shone in. The spiky-haired boy glared at me over his shoulder before getting up and leaving. Then another student barged in and retrieved something from under the desk. Mr. Dukakis muttered something to him about homework being due on Friday, no excuses.

What would happen if you didn't turn your homework in? Nothing. Not a goddamn thing in this world would happen, except that a teacher with a brain that was two cans short of a six pack would scribble in red ink that you were an idiot.

At last, we were alone.

"Good morning," Mr. Dukakis said, his stony expression roving the classroom, even though it was only the three of us. "Thank you for coming."

"I'm Jenna."

"My," Mr. Dukakis looked at me. "Your safety patrol vest takes me back to the kind we wore when I was your age."

For some reason, I was nervous even with a gun in my shorts, and I followed Jenna's suggestion to shut up and drink my drink.

Mr. Dukakis stuck a ballpoint pen behind his ear and locked the classroom door.

"If you don't mind," he said. "I'd like to get this over with. How should we proceed?"

Jenna stood from the desk with the stiffness and authority of a case worker sent to a group home on a holiday. She lifted a pile of clothes out of the Eastpak. Mr. Dukakis seemed to know what it was, and then I caught on, too, 'cuz I'm no dummy. Children's shirts, shoes, dresses; picked through from other dirty rotten markets and sold and passed around in the backs of trucks and dirty rotten "online" places.

"I've never done anything like this before," Mr. Dukakis said, his face reddening shamefully.

"I want $5K for the loot," Jenna said.

I swallowed the lump in my throat. The pervert looked winded, like he might fall down and hurt himself.

"I have cash," he said.

"You better."

I took a big gulp of chocolate milk, watching Mr. Dukakis comb through socks and fringy dresses and blue denim with sand caked in the knees. Some of the t-shirts were smudged or dirty. He lifted a plain red t-shirt from the pile and breathed it in, running a hand over the sodden collar.

"It reminds me," he said.

Jenna said, "You're lucky we're not in the parking lot of a dollar store where you could run into your wife."

"I appreciate the timely arrangement." He gulped, lifting a belt with the Powerpuff Girls in the pink stitching. "I'm not what you think. Heather—she was a student of mine."

"Where did she sit?" I asked.

"She sat in the first row, over there," Mr. Dukakis gestured. "We've kept the desk empty so it's hers when she returns."

"How sentimental," Jenna snickered.

Mr. Dukakis smiled, shrugging pitifully. "The whole world's messed up and I'm broken myself. I can't help who or what I am, but I know I'm doing my best."

"You're a pervert, Mr. Dukakis. A guy like you is how I stay in business." She reached into the Eastpak and pulled out a girl's athletic shoe, white and green with blades of grass stains in the rubber folds. "Do you know who this belonged to?"

Mr. Dukakis shut his eyes, his hands trembling, like Olivia's in the restroom when she saw the handgun.

"I don't know," he said.

"I think you do," said Jenna.

"How do I know you're not—pulling my leg?" Mr. Dukakis asked. He nervously took the ballpoint pen from behind his ear and slapped it into his palm.

"You don't. You either recognize the shoe or you don't. She sat right in front of you all school year, you'd think you'd know—"

"Okay," Mr. Dukakis said. "I recognize it. Yes. Please, just don't be so rough with me. I'll take it off your hands."

Jenna piled everything together–even the athletic shoe–back inside the bag. He looked like he was on the verge of terrified tears.

"My wife," he laughed. "My wife is so scared about the new millennium; how, digitally, the year 2000 will affect our computer systems. She's mad, my wife is. She told me this story once about being abducted by aliens while she was on vacation with her family at Gulf Shores. Aliens. Sometimes all you can do is laugh and pray. I'm thinking of returning to church. I'm dreaming about Heather Studebaker every night that she's not returned safely to her mother. I'm a good man. I'm a good man. I am. I'm a good man."

Mr. Dukakis handed Jenna a manila envelope filled with cash. She counted it, fast, and then stuffed it down her pants. She sniffled, then laughed. "Does your wife know you're meeting with a teenage girl on your lunch break?"

Mr. Dukakis was handling a small transparent baggie. From where I sat, it looked like a bag of seashells.

"They're teeth," he said. "From whom?"

"From Whoever-the-Fuck," said Jenna. "I took them out of somebody's mouth yesterday. You want them–that'll be another $300."

I looked down at my own fingernail beds, still beaded with the blood I knocked out of Stu. It was harder than it looked, hitting somebody. I was still in pain, although I'd rather shoot myself in the head with the handgun than admit it to Jenna.

Mr. Dukakis started crying. His eyes weren't just swollen, but real tears came, and the sharpness of his whimper only grew as he held another man's broken teeth, ridges caked in blood, close to his face to see them up close.

"Like what you see? It always costs you," Jenna said.

"Let me get my pocketbook."

Unfortunately, for me, there was more to hand over than just the teeth. Mr. Dukakis wanted my t-shirt: D.A.R.E. To Keep Kids off Drugs. He told Jenna that if I gave him the shirt off my back, he wouldn't forget his manners and tattle to the authorities that we were up to dirty, rotten, no good things.

"Cute bargain. Do it," said Jenna, to me.

"I don't wanna," I said. "I'm not taking my shirt off."

"Do it. You don't want me taking it off you myself."

Mr. Dukakis focused sharply on me as I took the vest off, letting it fall to the floor. I glared at Jenna as I took off the D.A.R.E. shirt and tossed it to Mr. Dukakis. My sunburns were splotched open, maybe infected. Mr. Dukakis watched me the entire time. I was fast. I put the bright orange vest back on, focusing on my shoes. The only sound was the ticking of the clock on the wall.

I glared at Jenna. She pantomimed me, mouthing "what" as if I was the biggest dummy on earth. "You don't wanna start with me," she said.

"Thank you for your time," Mr. Dukakis said. He turned his back on the two of us, the clothes bundled in his arms, small socks, my t-shirt, a fringy dress, overalls. Kidnapped Heather's sneaker. "Please, please leave. Go on. Please go. I mean it. Before I call security."

There I was, shirtless, dumb, broke, the crusty moles on my back exposed and itching in patches around a sunburn. No money on me. Jenna didn't even give me the five bucks she promised. On the way out of the school, I wanted to kill them all, especially Mr. Dukakis.

CHAPTER TWELVE

Bradford County Corrections Department
INTERROGATION SUBJECT: Ms. Jenna Ramos
DATE: May 27, 1999, 11:10 PM
INTERVIEWED BY: Detective Brian Bower
DETECTIVE NOTE: 3 weeks prior to Studebaker abduction

DETECTIVE BOWER: Jenna Ramos, resident of 417 Jackass Crossing Rd. Yeehaw Junction, Florida. We have a lot to cover. I know you're shaken up by being brought here in a police cruiser but I'm going to tell you right now, you're not booked, you're not even in trouble. Not with me.

JENNA RAMOS: Okay.

DETECTIVE BOWER: I can tell you're a good kid and I don't want to see you get hurt, so that's why I'm talking to you today and I'm hoping you can give me some information. Kill two birds with one stone–how's that?

JENNA RAMOS: Okay.

DETECTIVE BOWER: First of all, I've read you your rights. You are a minor, and in the state of Florida you do not need a guardian present for this interrogation. I'd like, however, to notify a parent or a guardian of what transpired today, but we can get to that later on. First of all, Jenna, how old are you?

JENNA RAMOS: I'm sixteen.

DETECTIVE BOWER: What grade are you in?

JENNA RAMOS: I'm on honor roll at Kissimmee High School.

DETECTIVE BOWER: Congratulations, good for you. You like school? Does it come easy to you or do you have to study really hard to be on the honor roll?

JENNA RAMOS: Both, I think. I'm smart but I also study.

DETECTIVE BOWER: Terrific. Okay, Jenna, you're sixteen, you're on the honor roll, you've got a big family at home with a brother. You live in Yeehaw Junction, is that correct?

JENNA RAMOS: Yes.

DETECTIVE BOWER: Okay, tell me about what happened today, May 27, 1999?

JENNA RAMOS: I got in trouble for trespassing at the park.

DETECTIVE BOWER: You got in trouble for trespassing in a no access zone at a state park. Do you know the name of it?

JENNA RAMOS: Withlacoochee State Forest.

DETECTIVE BOWER: What else did you get in trouble for today? Think really hard.

JENNA RAMOS: I walked out of an Ace Hardware with stuff I didn't pay for. I meant to pay for it, but when I realized I was already walking to the parking lot, I panicked and just kept going. So, they caught me.

DETECTIVE BOWER: Right. I appreciate your honesty. You walked outside with unpaid merchandise. You had the intention to pay for it, but you decided at the last minute to just see if you could get away with it? You were already out the door.

JENNA RAMOS: Yeah. Basically, I didn't turn back when I realized what happened. I didn't think I'd get caught.

DETECTIVE BOWER: Tell me about what merchandise you walked out of the store with.

JENNA RAMOS: I can't remember.

DETECTIVE BOWER: Try really hard. I can refresh your memory for you. Let's see, you had four five-gallon paint buckets. You had a gallon of bleach. You had—

JENNA RAMOS: I had a bendy air duct—

DETECTIVE BOWER: That's right, you had a ventilation duct with you. Those move concentrated air from one space to another space, right? So, we've got the ventilation duct, four five-gallon paint buckets, a gallon of bleach, and a jug of pork rinds. The pork rinds, Jenna, I don't have a problem with that. Do you prefer pork rinds to Pringles?

JENNA RAMOS: I like pork rinds.

DETECTIVE BOWER: Good answer. Pork rinds are a superior snack. Okay, Jenna, can you tell me something? What were you planning to do with all of these stolen items? You're a smart young woman, you're sixteen, it's a Saturday, it's almost summer vacation. What were you planning to do once you got to Withlacoochee State Forest?

JENNA RAMOS: I was gonna paint the mining tractors.

DETECTIVE BOWER: Okay, so you were headed for the mining quarry—I'm assuming the mining quarry within Withlacoochee—

JENNA RAMOS: Yeah.

DETECTIVE BOWER: —with paint buckets and bleach. Have you hiked that trek into the quarry before?

JENNA RAMOS: I can't remember. I don't think so. I know about it because somebody at school was talking about it. They said there was a lot of mining equipment left behind, like excavators and diggers, stuff like that. I thought it would be cool to just go and hang out and be alone, and paint over everything.

DETECTIVE BOWER: And did you see the No Trespassing signs upon arriving to that area of the forest?

JENNA RAMOS: Yeah, I did. But I also saw a sign that said Foot Traffic Only, so I thought it wasn't the worst thing in the world.

DETECTIVE BOWER: Okay, that's fair. So, it's just you, nobody else is with you?

JENNA RAMOS: I'm by myself.

DETECTIVE BOWER: Okay, Jenna, like I said, I don't want to see you get hurt. The quarry is dangerous. In fact, it's one of the most dangerous places in the state of Florida, as far as I'm concerned. A lot of hikers like to make the jump off the limestone—huge jump—and hit the water, and what happens is, Jenna, they hit that water not realizing that there's old machinery down in the water, the dozers, like you mentioned. There's broken wheels, broken stairs. There's so much damage. It's a death trap, is what it is. The spring at that quarry looks deep, and sometimes it is, and a few feet more, it's shallow as the day is long. You understand?

JENNA RAMOS: Yeah.

DETECTIVE BOWER: You're out there by yourself, you decide to take a swim, or you climb up a metal staircase that's littered with nature, you can't see, you can't see where you're going—you drop. If you drop, Jenna, that's it. You hit your head, that's it. It's very dangerous. Had you planned to hike all the way up there with the paint buckets in each hand? That seems like a hopeless venture.

JENNA RAMOS: I figured I could leave the paint someplace and remember where it was, if the hike was too long or too steep. I'd come back for it. Like, carry one paint gallon at a time or something.

DETECTIVE BOWER: Interesting. You must be strong.

JENNA RAMOS: I didn't think it through all the way. I was going to figure it out on the hike.

DETECTIVE BOWER: That gives us a lot to think about, certainly. I'd like to ask you a question, Jenna, and I want you to think about it before you give me an answer. You can sit and ruminate on it all day, if you want to. We're not under a time crunch.

JENNA RAMOS: Okay.

DETECTIVE BOWER: Do you know anyone by the name of Angel Stanton?

JENNA RAMOS: No.

DETECTIVE BOWER: Think about it.

JENNA RAMOS: I am thinking about it, but, no, unless Angel's in one of my classes and I don't know them. Sometimes kids transfer in or out.

DETECTIVE BOWER: Okay. Tell us about your foster mother. Do you have a good relationship with her?

JENNA RAMOS: Yeah, Trudy's pretty cool. We get along. She works a lot.

DETECTIVE BOWER: Well, two kids is a lot to look after.

JENNA RAMOS: Yeah.

DETECTIVE BOWER: It's you, your older brother, Macon—who else?

JENNA RAMOS: It's just the two of us and Trudy's retarded sister.

DETECTIVE BOWER: A developmentally disabled sister, okay.

JENNA RAMOS: Yeah.

DETECTIVE BOWER: You have a nice relationship with everybody in the home?

JENNA RAMOS: Pretty much. Sometimes Macon and I fight, but it's not as bad as it used to be.

DETECTIVE BOWER: Sibling rivalry never skips a generation.

JENNA RAMOS: Yeah.

DETECTIVE BOWER: Okay, Jenna. You're a good student, a good kid, you're conscientious, at least in my eyes. What we have here is some botched shoplifting, less than $150 worth of merchandise. Let's not do that again. Trespassing. Trespassing is dangerous, especially for a young woman. The mining quarry is not safe. Your peers don't know what they're talking about. Don't listen to them.

JENNA RAMOS: Okay.

DETECTIVE BOWER: Jenna, tell me right now. What were you planning to do in the quarry today?

JENNA RAMOS: Nothing. I told you already; paint and chill out.

DETECTIVE BOWER: I don't believe you.

JENNA RAMOS: It's the truth.

DETECTIVE BOWER: The tendency of most teenagers is to lie, let's get that right off the bat. You're lying and I know that because a sixteen-year-old girl doesn't go on hikes in the 92-degree humidity at the start of summer into a mining quarry, with stolen paint and bleach, and not have some pretext. A hike you've never taken in your life, I might add. Something's not adding up.

JENNA RAMOS: It's the truth.

DETECTIVE BOWER: And the ventilation duct? What about that?

JENNA RAMOS: I was gonna use it to vacuum out any excess leaves. It's faster that way.

DETECTIVE BOWER: How is it faster?

JENNA RAMOS: It collects more.

DETECTIVE BOWER: Did you bring a vacuum with you to the park?

JENNA RAMOS: No, I never got that far. I didn't think about it until I had already left Ace Hardware.

DETECTIVE BOWER: One more time. Do you know somebody named Angel Stanton and did you see him today in the forest?

JENNA RAMOS: No, and no.

CHAPTER THIRTEEN

JUNE 25, 1999. It started at the payphone, as all phone calls do. I'll tell you about how I got from sitting in a booth at Kmart with some no good, bad twenty-somethings; to being facedown in the Salida Preserve with mud and grit on my neck and what I thought was the moonlight hanging over me, naked (shirtless) as the day I was born in the trash can.

I ended up not committing mass murder because I never made it to the piggy station. I had bigger problems to weed through than worry about where Trudy was. After Mr. Dukakis gave Jenna the cash for the clothes, Jenna left me fending for myself. She got into a car with a friend of Ziggy's. I walked by myself all the way from the middle school to a strip mall bumming people for change. There was a payphone between a tag-and-title and a pain clinic, and I needed to make a call.

The moms took less pity on me than the sick people in slippers walking into the pain clinic. Nobody wanted to talk to a gap-toothed kid looking like something the cat dragged in from the short bus.

After twenty minutes of spare-changing with no luck, I gave up and snatched a quarter out of a bum's cup. He was so out of it I don't think he noticed. The fact of the matter was, me and Cricket had been homeless, too, but not for long. It didn't mean you were without a roof. It meant you didn't have an address. Big difference.

At the payphone, I dialed Starr's phone number. I'd had it memorized for a long time but never called that wackjob until today. It rang four times before she finally picked up, sounding as breathless and out of it as the bum with the quarter and no place to be. She pretended not to know who I was, or why the hell I'd call her.

I threw a tantrum, cursing, screaming, walloping into the pay phone until saliva dripped down my chin. Men shook their heads at my outburst, women averted their eyes, people rolled down their car windows to hear better. Everybody was annoyed at me for being on the phone. Everybody was annoyed at me for being mad. Why does a young white man have to act like that? Where was my mama? Sure, I could've pulled out Cricket's Survivor Day handgun and blown somebody's head off. But instead I looked directly into the receiver, like they do in the movies.

Starr, she started hollering, too. "Call me again and I'm callin' the police! I don't know you! I don't know why–"

"Yes, you do! Yes, you do!"

"Fuck you!"

"I'm Skeet! Trudy's in the slammer and I need a ride to get her out!"

"Hang up this goddamn phone."

"I'm a long ways from Yeehaw, out where you live! I need a ride!" I screamed that last word–ride.

A woman stormed out of the pain clinic, an unlit cigarette dangling from her lip. She raised her arms in the air, shouted for me to hit the road and quit flipping out.

"Your mouth needs soap, boy!" she said.

"Don't it, though!"

People's voices started rising. Two smelly dudes slammed the pay phone down for me. They hustled me, sent me on my way. I told them they didn't know who they were dealing with. I stomped away, shooting everybody a middle finger.

"Suck it!" I said, and left.

Kmart was across the street so I hoofed it over there, hungry, shirtless except for the orange rescue vest. I started thinking about the time Starr got hepatitis. It was one of those diseases with a diagnosis class—A, B, C, one of them. Trudy refused to fuck Starr on their mattress until she quit coughing up blood. Maybe, I thought, the hepatitis went to her brain and that was why she was behaving like a psycho bitch, not helping me bail Trudy out, pretending not to know who I was. I didn't like being messed with.

Fuck Starr. Fuck Marilyn Manson. Fuck Mr. Dukakis. Fuck this vest. Fuck Kidnapped Heather. Fuck Jenna. Fuck Olivia. Fuck Trudy. Fuck the schools. Fuck the cunt at the pain clinic. Fuck those white bread freaks bleeding out in our bathroom. Fuck the new millennium. Fuck it all to hell.

At the Kmart, I went to the diner and swiped an RC Cola from the cooler. I sat in a brown vinyled booth. Sweat poured off me. I took a whiff of my own armpits. I smelled like jambalaya left sitting out too long. Some college-aged suckers introduced themselves and joined me in the booth. They ordered me a cheeseburger and fries from a frumpy waitress. Why? Well, I couldn't tell you that, not yet. I don't like talking to most people because most people got nothing to say, but like all things on this day, shit changed and I had no way to get where I needed to be. All I had on me was the vest and the gun.

I don't remember their names, although they told me. It went in one ear and out the other, just like when they told me they were criminology majors at UF. These suckers had their biceps tattooed with tribal bands. Their parents were probably married, middle-class bitches, who named their kids with the aim that they'd grow up and be somebody special and get filthy rich if they hustled hard enough, farting out I Voted! stickers every presidential election. Somebody at some point had given a shit.

There was a dude named Kim; I remember that much. The chick that sat next to him had a Hope 4 Heather button clipped over her left tit, with the other chick—I'll call her Steph. Steph wore a baby tank with The Offspring album cover of a rude little boy getting eaten by a locust. The other guy was so forgettable, I couldn't pick him out of a crowd.

Kim told me they spotted me pitching a fit across the street. They tapped their temples concerningly, wanting the little details of my black eye and no shirt. (Whatever happened to "No shoes, no shirt, no problem"?)

"You a scrapper?" Steph asked. She smiled deviously. It was the same look Starr had the last time I saw her on Trudy's mattress, sprawled out without pants because she didn't know I was peeking.

There was a reason nobody trusted girls.

Like a sucker, I reported all about Starr not giving me a ride back to Yeehaw Junction and pretending she didn't know me even though she'd been dating Trudy for forever. I told them that it made her an even bigger cunt than Heather Studebaker was for hiding out all this time. I said that I knew Starr had abducted Heather, too. I knew everybody's secrets. Steph asked if Starr was my girlfriend, and there was some giggling and elbowing among the four of them. Kim drummed his fingers on the back of the vinyl booth, apologizing for the others' laughter. He said the reason they sat down with me was because I looked like I could use some lunch.

"And a shirt and tie, maybe," Steph said.

"You could use some calamine lotion on those burns," the one chick said. "You ever heard of sunscreen?"

"You ever heard of DDT soil? I sell it. Two dollars a jar." The four of them sniggered. "I'm not supposed to talk about it, but I also work for Marilyn Manson."

More sniggering. Steph elbowed the forgettable dude.

"You hear that?" the forgettable dude smiled. "Scrapper's a businessman for Marilyn Manson. You must be one smart puppy."

"I am," I said.

Suddenly, a waitress in a big apron brought me over a cheeseburger, fries, and a goddamn, good as gold milkshake. I devoured the food, double-fisting fries, smearing ketchup on the sides of the tray.

"See, you were hungry," Kim said.

"I'm Skeet."

"Hi, Skeet." They said it in unison, like they really meant it.

Steph gave me a piggy-back ride down the CD aisle. I swiped candy. Kim said I was a laugh riot. The four of them even said they'd give me a ride. Next thing I knew, I was getting into their van. It seemed like a reasonable way to get out of town. Fun, even.

The ride was stuffy, a pedo van without windows and it stank like weed. The smell was as bad as Macon's socks when he came inside wearing his outside clothes.

Kim told me to pick my poison, but I didn't know what that shit meant. He changed his words. He asked me what my stimulant of choice was. We sat knee to knee for a few minutes while they took turns offering me pills and a flask.

I took one pill from them without question, washed it down with whiskey that burned so bad, I coughed like a pussy afterward. After the second drink, it burned again, and I shivered, feeling lightheaded, warm inside. After a few warm breaths, and another drink, I became the funniest man in the whole world. There was hooting and hollering, bare thigh clapping. Remarks ricocheted which I didn't understand a lick of. Steph asked me if I had a girlfriend and if I spent all my money on her.

"Nobody hangs out at a pain clinic without dough, Scrapper," Kim said.

Somebody drove. Well, the van was going somewhere. I didn't know for how long because my head was swimming and I was making the four of them laugh, almost pissing their pants.

"When you get your pain pills, Scrapper, how much money do you spend?" Steph asked.

Well, I didn't know what they were talking about because I was higher than a fucking kite. I plucked a joint from the chick with the sunglasses, taking a deep hit that lingered in a nice plume of smoke around us. I told them the only girlfriend I had was named Olivia. She was obsessed with me. She sucked my dick in the school bathroom but wouldn't fire a gun with me.

"Like, she was fucking friends with the missing girl. It makes you think," I said.

They agreed. It did make you think.

An hour into the van ride, I fell asleep but woke up suddenly, after having a dream about falling down the stairs. The four strangers were all just staring at me, speaking quietly to each other. I asked them if I could stay and be in their gang. I asked if I could live with them. I said I'd have to get back to Yeehaw Junction to pick up Cricket. No, she wasn't my sister, and she wasn't my mama, neither. She was pregnant and a business partner, and a friend. But she went with me wherever I went.

They laughed at her name, like they were laughing at everything else and still thought I was the funniest Florida man they'd ever smoked with.

"Why's her name Cricket?" Steph asked.

"It just is, is all," I said. "Some people are born to name themselves and ain't nothing wrong with it."

I passed out again. This time, I don't know for how long, but a bump in the road jolted me awake. All I could hear was thumping and giggling, and a nervous exclamation from Kim. He slammed on the brakes and the van tumbled and skidded as we flew off the main road and into the prairie. I barfed. Most of it got on the floor of the van, and one of the chicks screamed. I barfed a second time. Kim cut the engine, turned around in the driver's seat, and asked me if I knew where we were. I didn't have a clue but I hoped it was near Yeehaw Junction.

They got me. They got me good.

Steph gripped my hands behind my back as the forgettable, asshole dude thumbed through my vest pockets looking for cash. I tried biting his chin but I got a mouthful of his hair instead. They took my shoes off, which were the good shoes that Ziggy got for me when I pointed to a boy my age in the street and said, 'I want those shoes, the ones he has', and here I was, getting those chucks taken off me like they were taken off him. The chick took the chucks and banged them against the van as if a million dollars was going to come dripping out. Nothing did, of course. Except maybe the smell of my feet. Then they came for my camo pants. The Survivor's Day handgun flipped out of the waistband and hit the floor with a thud.

"What the fuck!"

"He's got a gun!" Steph said.

A unified panic filled the van. I demanded they give it back to me. The problem was, I was too dizzy and fatigued to do anything but lie there. Whiskey spilled on me, and one of them—I don't know which dude, maybe Kim—carried me out of the van. I didn't thrash, didn't even try to get out alive. I went face-down into the high grass, a speckle of sand dotting my forehead. I cursed at them, demanding my gun back.

"He's a little Columbine psycho," Steph said. "I'm not touching that!"

"Let's go!" The forgettable man clapped his hands. "By the way, Scrapper, Marilyn Manson's real name is Brian Warner and he's a fucking poser!"

The handgun and my shoes went flying into the grass. More commotion: van doors slammed and the exhaust smoked near my face as the four of them bugged out, spiraling about Tampa and the gun. I was too drugged out to see where my shit went, too tired to move. Frogs croaked, cicadas whistled, and full dark came. I fell fast asleep.

When I awoke, whenever that was, it was pitch black except for the moon shining down on me like an angel. An orb like a big eye judging me. Wanted to kill 'em all and the big guy upstairs still sent me an angel. Grass as far as my good eye could see. I was still shirtless. My shoes got thrown one way; the handgun, the most important thing, the other way. I turned my head on my stiff-ass neck.

The old man in the black trench coat stood over me under the moon. We stared at each other. He was unblinking and serious, with a quivering jowl and small black eyeglasses like before. This time it was only the two of us. He didn't come close to my face, but I could feel his breath, feel him whisper in my ear: "Radium and lead in youngblood's head. Everything goes to hell."

Black shadows clouded my vision like the pot smoke in the van. I tripped on whatever dreamspace this was, whatever crazy thing was happening to me in the moonlight, me and the man in black. I closed my eyes and saw a vision of Kidnapped Heather, but there were clouds between us, sinkholes as cavernous as the moles on my skin. I gasped, shooting up from the grass.

Kidnapped Heather was alive and close by. I'd find her and get rich.

It was a rough walk back to Yeehaw Junction. I carried my wet chucks because it was easier that way. I dodged shallow potholes in the pouring rain, stomping through floodwater along the I-60 guardrail as a blister pulsed on my big toe. Handgun back in my shorts. I got honked at a few times. I felt like my skull was going to split open from the throbbing in my head. When I walked past the pylons and over the fence, somebody was crying up the ways. Only a shaft of light from the vacant barn across the road lit up the lonely street. Nobody was outside. I ran as fast as my legs would pump, holding the handgun against my thigh so it wouldn't budge from the camo shorts.

A shrill scream, a door slammed. Some horrible guttural bark that I wasn't half certain came from a human was coming out of our house. All the lights were on at our place, even the shed light way in the back. I could see the inflatable pool filled with rain and leaves, where Macon had bought the farm.

"Cricket?" I said.

Blood. Not everywhere, but a trail of blood emerging from the Florida-room and leaking onto the porch, dripping off the steps and into the grass. Cricket's No Fear t-shirt was covered in blood and so was whatever she was holding. For a minute, I thought the ground shook, like the whole house was about to come down.

"Cricket?"

My left eardrum went out as my heart pounded.

Cricket sat on the bottom step with the porch light shining on her. She held a slimy, white-powdered, pink and bloody baby in her arms. The tendril of umbilical cord was draped over her shoulder like a feather boa.

I dropped my chucks in the soaked grass. Bam Bam called my name from up in the tree, where he wasn't supposed to be. I hoofed it past Cricket, demanding to know what was going on. A puddle of blood led me into the bathroom where we left the two piggies. Mallory's intestines spilled out of her, and the hollow, bloody space below where the baby came out of. Stu was still next to her, tied up, gasping for air, slouched like a loser.

I smiled, a cascade of satisfaction sobering me up.

I joined Cricket on the porch step. Her hair was peppered with gore, but she was beaming with sheer happiness. She looked like a child holding a child.

"I had the baby, Skeet. Finally."

CHAPTER FOURTEEN

Skeeter Syndrome Outbreak at Kissimmee Middle School
Central Florida Sentinel, 04/08/99
by Neil Doran

Kissimmee Park Middle School in Kissimmee is experiencing one of the worst outbreaks of what is known as 'skeeter syndrome' that's ever been reported. Skeeter syndrome is an inflammatory reaction to mosquito bites, and although it's rare and doesn't typically warrant treatment outside of over-the-counter topical creams, some health authorities are calling it a Central Florida epidemic. Outdoor P.E., student sports, and all after-school activities are canceled for the remainder of the month, and won't resume until May. Faculty is encouraging parents not to allow their child to walk to and from school during storm season months when mosquitos are thriving.

"If we can get this under control now and eliminate the possibilities of spreading it further, then our students and faculty can start the 1999/2000 school year healthy and ready to learn. We don't want to see a bunch of students unattended for the first few weeks in

September if preventative measures can be taken," Principal Lauren Myers said.

There's reason to believe that skeeter syndrome might affect middle schoolers differently because of hormonal changes. The primary carrier is one particularly nasty mosquito, derived from what may be an Evergladian eyesore of a recent cluster in Central Florida. Skeeter syndrome symptoms include a reddening rash that doesn't clear in 1-3 days, worsening itchy or skin peeling, skin warmth at the exposure site, swelling, blisters, pocks, and if with a weakened immune system, fever.

Twenty-four students have been diagnosed since March 14 but are expected to make a full recovery.

CHAPTER FIFTEEN

JUNE 28, 1999. Jenna shook a cigarette from my pack, lit up, and exhaled. She squatted in the middle of one of Mallory's bloodstains. There was a whiff of bleach in the air. Cradling the camcorder, she opened the panel with her chin, told me to keep going, don't stop.

Intertwining his swollen fingers gently in mine, I nibbled on Stu's fingernails. I peeled off the little pale fingernail with my teeth, sticking my tongue out to show it. I picked the nail off my tongue, showed it to the camera. I knew what Jenna was doing. She was zooming into my face, getting close-ups of the fingernail, again and again.

"Is he dead?" Jenna asked, still recording. I could tell because the red light was on.

"I dunno."

Zooming, close-ups of my face.

Jenna turned slightly to the right, panning over Stu. He may as well have been dead, except his chest still moved up and down. Sometimes a deep, guttural moan emitted from his stinky mouth. His neck pulsed. His skin had turned a shade of grape purple like the brat in Willy Wonka and the Chocolate Factory. I'd played with his other hand all morning, holding the broken fingers in my hand, one after the other. Bastard would never flip anybody the bird ever again.

"What happened to *her* body?" I meant the other towhead, and Jenna knew what I meant, but she didn't answer me right away.

More close-ups of the broken fingers.

"Jenna," I said. "'Radium and lead in youngblood's head'–what's that mean?"

"I dunno."

"Do I look good?" I asked.

Jenna didn't give me an answer. I guess it didn't matter. The red dot flickered on the camcorder's panel. Jenna's cigarette ashes sprinkled around the bloodstain. I reached over the edge of the bathtub, picking up Stu's other hand, squeezing it in my fist so the creases in his knuckles turned purple.

Piggie was still breathing.

I used my imagination about what happened to Mallory's body. Somebody came for her while we were asleep. Stuffed her in a wheelbarrow, pulled her through this hellish, hot landscape, and chucked her into Buttermilk Slough where she floated to Cockroach Creek and worms squirmed upon her body in the ditch. Somebody would come for Stu, too, once he was dead.

Trudy was coming back today, and I'd show her my life's work: the blood, what bones I'd broken, the way I carried us all through it, and the footage we got.

In our happy abode, sunbeams struck the shopping carts in neat splits. The summer had already yellowed the corners of the Will Smith centerfold. Cricket wore a polyester pink t-shirt with a grinning white bunny rabbit holding an assault rifle with *Y24 Got Me* in raised, sparkly lettering. There was a butterfly clipped to the top of her head. Old strands of Mallory's long, blond, coconut-scented hair hung down in front of Cricket's face, like a badge of honor. Cricket chopped it herself after she was done cutting the baby out of Mallory, at least that's what Jenna told me. Jenna thought Cricket wearing the dead woman's hair was a step too far.

Cricket named the baby Lil Rascal. She was the best mama in the whole world. The high-pitched screams barking out of that little thing didn't even bother Cricket in the middle of the night, at any hour, not once. She loved that baby so much. Lil Rascal was covered in blood and a white, layered powder on its skin when it was born, looking like it climbed out of a grave.

In a way, it did.

Me and Cricket didn't care about Lil Rascal's gender because its hoo-hoo didn't tell us nothing about what that baby was gonna turn out to be. No coochie or dick and balls can tell you that. Nobody gives a fuck. I sure don't. If you do, you're a pervert. If you're a pervert, you might as well be dead.

Cricket's big tits dangled in front of Lil Rascal's mouth even though milking those things was out of the question. Tell that to Cricket and she'd pitch a fit. She'd give us the reminder that breast-feeding consumes 25 percent of the mama's energy, so it wasn't nice to say to a new mama that was trying her best. Ziggy bought newborn formula off a grandma that lived next door to his ex, and, boy, oh, boy, could Lil Rascal suck down formula like it was going out of style. It looked like regular milk from the farm store. Cricket dribbled her nipples with the stuff to make it feel like she was leaking all over the place.

"All a baby needs is mama's milk," said Cricket, tucking a chunk of Mallory's hair behind her ear. It immediately fell back in front of her face. "It sleeps after it's fed."

"Sure does, Cricket," I said.

"Sure," Jenna said, flopping into the loveseat, still smoking her cigarette. "A newborn doesn't need to be swaddled, belched, changed, fed, everything that none of you know how to do or half-ass." She rolled her eyes, seizing the clicker from beneath the cushion. "None of this was supposed to happen. We had a different plan. Cable's out—*fuck*."

Cricket made kissy faces at the baby.

"Guess what, little one?" Cricket said. "We're going to Gatorzone today. Trudy's escaping the slammer and we're all going to meet at the Gator Motor Lodge. It's your first trip ever."

I hovered over Lil Rascal in the old-school Fisher Price baby carriage, looking at its weird little hairs, listening to the wheezing sound that occasionally came out of its tooter. I flopped Stu's finger in front of its face. The finger had changed shades so much since getting lopped off it looked almost rubber, blue, not soft.

"Can you grab the finger?" I said. "Can you grab the finger?"

I touched Lil Rascal's fingers to Stu's fingers, making a V.

"See what you made us do?" Jenna said, rolling her eyes.

She tried the T.V. one more time.

§

First stop, the alligator capital of the world: Gatorzone. Me, Cricket, Lil Rascal, Bam Bam, and Jenna hitchhiked half the way to Orange Blossom Trail and hopped the bus the rest of the way. Orlando was eight miles through the deep swamp south's small intestine. I didn't know the temperature but the strawberry farmer that got us there told us to watch our steps.

And much to her confoundment, we met Starr at the Gatorzone entrance by the belly of the beast. I glared at her and she glared at me like a deer in fucking headlights. The stupid bitch got her shifts back after probation. I just wanted Trudy back. I'd do whatever got Trudy out of the slammer faster, even if it meant parading around with Starr for the afternoon until she could hook us up with a ride.

The entry to Gatorzone was in the shape of a slime green toothed gator's open mouth. It was supposed to look like the gator was taking a bite out of you. *SINCE 1949*. I photobombed tourists taking pictures in front of it, making bunny ears and middle fingers, rude, crude tongues.

A tourist asked me who I was and I said, "I'm a scumbag."

The tourist told me to get a life, get lost.

Starr wasn't too happy seeing a baby on Cricket's chest. Whose baby was it, what was it doing here, what did we think we were doing with it. Her curses whipped us with the who, what, where, why, fuck, and how. Jenna took the heat while I snatched a beach towel from a rack and blanketed it over Lil Rascal's body, nuzzled in the crick of Cricket's shoulder.

"I trust you're ditching town," Starr said, when we got to the noisy aviary. "I practically got pounded at that scary precinct."

"How about let's not talk about trust," Jenna said. "I've collected these three scumbags–*four*–and now I'm leaving them with you. They're not coming with me."

"Well, they're not coming with *me*!"

"Quiet your trap. Aren't you on the fucking clock?" Jenna said. "Go to work."

Starr scoffed, storming off in her Gatorzone apron to ticket sales.

I didn't know what they were talking about and didn't care much. Trudy would sort it out. Give 'em hell.

Gatorzone had a domineering reek of sunscreen, BO, and wet labrador. Cricket was worried the birds in the aviary would swoop and yank Lil Rascal away, so we crossed the bridge to the sun-drenched dunes where rattlesnakes and cottonmouths lived like kings. There was a small valley to side-step a pebbled creek where every tourist from here to Toledo stopped to take a stupid picture.

I snapped my gums at a little girl wearing a sunhat, standing next to her distracted mama. They looked down from the pedestrian bridge, pointing at the snakes as if they were gonna get up and dance.

"Hiya," I said. She looked at me like she was looking right through me, seeing me for what I was, bad to the bone, bad inside, the boy with no color in his eyes. "Watch. He's gonna get you. Cottonmouths, they snap."

We visited the capybaras and the tortoise habitats. We watched the tourists in helmets zip-line over the marshes, the sun in our eyes. In the arena, we got some shade as a man wrestled an eight foot alligator in the sand. At the crocodile swamp, I talked shit to the tarantulas and barnyard animals by the ice cream pen. When it was time for the boat ride, somebody on the edge of the bridge vomited and fell down from heat stroke.

"Would you look at that," I said, lighting a dirty 305 I bummed off the strawberry farmer. "Some people can't take the heat."

"I think Lil Rascal likes the animals," Cricket said. "Can you take our picture?"

"We don't got a camera," I said. "Next time, Cricket."

"Okay, Skeet."

And then, in the heat and bustle of the crowd, the man in black appeared. His trenchcoat gave him away, the quivering jowl, the lonely eyes behind the black eyeglasses. A creeper. I was beginning to think he was a creeper. Everybody passed right by him. Nobody cared, but I stopped to look. He locked eyes with me, leaning over the murky water as if to see his reflection or a fish piddling by. The little girl in the sunhat sucked on a melting lemon popsicle, pointing to a creature moving in the water.

I moved cautiously through the crowd toward the man in black. A sharp current tickled the pink and red welts on my hand. It was like electricity but softer. Still burned.

"Where did you go?" I said.

Cricket called me back over to the boat ramp.

I ignored Cricket, maybe for the first time ever. She called again, louder this time, but I pushed through the crowd toward the man in black, toward the little girl on the bridge, toward the gator pad. I glanced at my pink and red welted hand, rubbing it against my pants and the rescue vest to cool it off.

Cricket called for me again.

I took Stu's finger out of my vest pocket. I'd cleaned it up real nice before we left and swiped it with some fabric softener. I'd bitten the fingernails down to nothing. It looked like a dog's chew toy. "Wanna see something?"

The way the little girl looked at me, she reminded me of Olivia. She didn't want to look, you could tell, but she couldn't help it.

"Mister Gator, eat the finger. Come on, Mister Gator." I got on my tip-toes and dangled the finger over the lily pads and bogs. "Mister Gator–"

I listened to my own heartbeat in my eardrum. I licked my bottom lip. I tossed the finger over as an albino gator charged from the bog like fucking Godzilla out of the Pacific, attacking that finger in one bite. Everybody clapped. Somebody congratulated me. As the feeding frenzy picked up, and the other gators emerged from the freshwater, I got the hell out of there, winking at the little girl, still pretending she was Olivia.

Cricket's face was a blubbery mess of snot and tears when I got back. The baby's beach towel was missing and it was fussing against her arms.

"Skeet," she cried. "I didn't know where you were! Me and Lil Rascal looked!"

I took Lil Rascal in my arms, even though baby holding was for girls. I didn't much like apologizing but I could see Cricket was shaken up.

"Sorry, Cricket," I said. "I fed the albinos."

Cricket blew her nose into the polyester pink bunny rabbit t-shirt. "Don't leave me, Skeet."

"I won't. You can count on that shit. Hey, look at me. I ain't never leaving."

The afternoon hours ticked by, the sun getting hotter, people dropped like weeds in the park because they weren't from the South and didn't know squat about hydrating like a horse in a race. Jenna fished us out of the crowd, though, filming what could only be a close-up of me walking down the sidewalk past the Holy Land Experience where Jesus Christ himself built a theme park.

As we walked into Waffle House, an American flag was beating off in the wind on the flagpole. *Hope 4 Heather* on the marquee, right next to the *2 for 1 Waffles*. Smoking or non-smoking? Smoking.

Something for everybody, I thought.

The air conditioning was a relief when we got to our seats. The paper menus at Waffle House were in the shape of Florida. Yeehaw Junction wasn't on the map. And why would it be? We didn't matter once in our lives, why would it be any different at the Waffle House with the smell of syrup, coffee, and fryer smoke up our noses? Too much white trash in our bathwater for anybody to care.

Me, Cricket, Lil Rascal, and Bam Bam sat on one side of the booth, Starr and Jenna on the other. Starr ordered chicken and waffles for all of us. And because I was no fuckhead, I voiced my skepticism about the Discman Jenna gifted me right there at the table, after watching her and Starr go at it about the cost of a train ticket after the waitress took our order. (The waitress also told all of us to lower our voices, she didn't need this today.)

The Discman was almost shiny; round, silver like our VCR, buttons over the translucent corners and attached were a pair of fuzzy black headphones. Bigger than they looked on T.V.

I flipped the lid of the Discman and there was a CD inside. Marilyn Manson. *Mechanical Animals.* Last time I held a Discman, it was Ziggy's. He socked me in the gut for dropping his Cypress Hill CD in the river.

"This a bribe?" I asked.

As a matter of fact, it was a bribe, because Jenna, glaring daggers into Lil Rascal, informed me that despite the heat wave I was gonna be slinging Hope 4 Heather merch at the crosswalk after Waffle House.

"T-shirts are five dollars," Jenna said. "Sell the whole crate or no Trudy."

"How long I got?" I asked.

"Not long."

Cricket pawed at the Discman and said, "Can I try it out?" Bam Bam suggested it was stolen from Service Merchandise, where we'd been banned since '95. I listened to Jenna and Starr's bickering, wanting to put a bullet in both of them, then fit the fuzzy black headphones over my head to drown out the fighting. Before the chicken and waffles came, I promptly took two Adderall with a cup of coffee–Adderall that I'd swiped from Ziggy. I wouldn't need sleep for days. On the T.V. in the corner of the kitchen, I could see the fry cook watching breaking news on Kidnapped Heather. They were always looking for somebody. I turned up my music as loud as it would go. I didn't want to hear the news.

Outside of the Gator Motor Lodge, I set up my selling post on the median of a four-lane highway. I had a crate full of t-shirts and a few glass jars of DDT soil. This was a way to make a living. Take no shit, punch hard, live like you're going to die because you gotta work for what little you can get, even in places that didn't have you on the map.

The rest of the afternoon shone so brightly, my face was hot to the touch. Starr instructed me to wait until the traffic light flipped red, then walk between the cars shouting biblically about Hope 4 Heather. Well, lucky for me, I was a born salesman and knew how to make a buck. Yesterday, Cricket and I spent hours stuffing new jars full of the soil. I'd offer 'em to anybody that was stupid enough to buy a t-shirt with a missing girl's face on it; the American way, as American as Mickey Mouse or food stamps you can't buy hot food with.

A middle-aged baby boomer rolled her window down and offered me ten bucks to get something to eat. She didn't want a shirt. She didn't want a jar, either. I told her I liked Kentucky Fried Chicken. I put Kidnapped Heather's shirt over the rescue vest. A little blocking of the sun was better than nothing. Another middle-aged baby boomer at the traffic light, an old-timer, rolled her window down when I knocked on the glass. She didn't like my knuckles beating on the glass but I asked her, "Hiya, you got extra room for me and Cricket?"

"What does that mean?"

"Cricket. She's my friend. Maybe we can ride with you someplace? Where you headed?" I asked.

But the light changed, the baby boomer rolled up her window, and hit the gas harder than everybody else.

The thing was, I was feeling something in danger. I couldn't explain it. Never had felt it before, not like today. The feelings showed up outside of the Gator Motor Lodge when Starr got real serious about me selling t-shirts. I felt as powerful as I was ruthless. I waited for the man in black to return in one of the vehicles. I willed him to get me, to take me where he wanted me to be.

I was thanked by Good Samaritans driving over the speed limit, not sure where they were coming or going, fist pumping to Kidnapped Heather. Doing good for the world during summer vacation, and all of that. They said the things grown-ups say when they don't know what to say 'cuz they can't believe a girl's gone missing in this country.

"Seems they're looking to arrest somebody else now," a young guy on a bike rattled off. He handed me five bucks. I gave him the t-shirt. "Yeah, I heard it on the radio. Nice tunes, bro."

"Don't believe what you hear on news radio," I shrugged. "You gotta try the Discman out."

"I'll do that. Catch you later."

"Catch you later," I said.

By nightfall, the traffic was still heavy and I'd earned my keep. I sold out of every Hope 4 Heather t-shirt and DDT jar in the crate. I climbed the chain-link fence to join the others at the swimming pool at Gator Motor Lodge. There were green tiles and salmon-colored concrete graffitied with the Orange County area code, 407. People in hospital gowns sat outside of the motel rooms in wheelchairs while unattended children ran up and down the asphalt, playing on the stairs. Folks milled around. Around the corner from the swimming pool enclosure was an old citrus grove where some kids fed trash to a jumping fire. I watched it get wilder. In a courtyard near the manager's office, a shady man was walking around mumbling to himself. He wasn't intoxicated, he just didn't have nobody giving him an ear. The chlorine smelled like poop. It also smelled like piss and skunkweed.

Bam Bam and I raced around the edges of the pool, jumping into the deep end and splashing everybody until they got sick of it. Starr babysat Lil Rascal because Lil Rascal got sick. Turned so red it looked like a tomato rotting in the sun. I don't know what was wrong with it but Starr, she said she knew what happened, and it was that Lil Rascal was overheated. Cricket was having such a blast splishing and splashing in the swimming pool, she forgot about Lil Rascal until Jenna reminded her that Starr was coming back downstairs with the kid.

Heat, sun exposure, secondhand smoke, chlorine, everything that could ever happen to you. All breathing down your neck.

Starr was pissed at the whole thing with the baby, but it wasn't Lil Rascal's fault, not even a little bit. The baby had seemingly cooled off because it lost some of its tomato-red color. Hell, it even looked like it lost some weight, which was great. Starr asked me when was the last time it took a dump, but I couldn't remember.

We swam until the motel manager made us leave, just as the sky turned the color of taffy. I'd share a room with Jenna and Ziggy on the second floor. It was the first time in my life that I'd ever had an entire bed to myself. I was a little scared, to tell you the truth. Not that I'd ever admit that to Starr or Jenna.

Under the covers, everything smelled clean. My skin still smelled of chlorine. I thumbed at the Discman, watching a commercial on MTV for Woodstock '99 in New York. Marilyn Manson flashed on the screen. I wanted to go to this Woodstock '99 thing and meet Marilyn Manson and start committing sick crimes with him.

Jenna and Ziggy got into a fight. Jenna even stormed out, slamming the door, but she banged on it to get right back in. When the two of them started fucking, I faced the wall. I could see their shadows humping, their hips and butts in the air, skin slapping. It would be the last time I'd ever see either two of them again, bodies bouncing into each other like wild animals. I put the fuzzy black headphones over my head, but the CD skipped every time my head hit the pillow.

As I was drifting off to sleep, something bit me in the big bed. I let it. I watched the thing slide up my arm and over the mole. I let it wrangle in the hairs and burrow into my skin, drawing blood. I let it take whatever it wanted.

CHAPTER SIXTEEN

YouTube Channel: "Strange and Unusual Florida"
Episode V

Published by user: January 28, 2010

Hey, everybody, and welcome back to my YouTube channel. I'm Craig and today I'm discussing more in-depth about one of my favorite places generally not found on a Florida map: Yeehaw Junction. Let's get started.

On August 10, 1981, two fishermen discovered a severed head in a drainage canal on the edge of Yeehaw Junction and the Florida Turnpike. The head belonged to that of poor Adam Walsh, a seven-year-old boy that had gone missing from Hollywood, Florida, just two weeks prior. A routine shopping trip with his mother at a Sears inside of a shopping mall spiraled into every parent's worst nightmare. Mom browsed the department store, Adam Walsh played with the new Atari 2600 video game console. Minutes later. He was gone.

He was kidnapped, strangled, and beheaded, allegedly by serial killer Ottis Toole. The rest of his body was never recovered.

The tragedy garnered national attention and panic about stranger abductions. Walsh's death ultimately changed how the United States dealt with heinous crimes against children. Adam's parents, Reve and Joe Walsh, assisted in creating the long-running series *America's Most Wanted*, bringing thousands of children home and their fugitives brought to justice. The FBI's NCIC National Crime Information Center established a database specifically for missing children. The federally-funded program, the National Center for Missing & Exploited Children, was established by 1984. The Child Protection & Safety Act updated and expanded the national sex offenders registry and national child abuse registry, in addition to the Survivors' Bill of Rights Act.

In 1994, federal buildings, military bases, and major retailers mobilized a missing child program called Code Adam, that prioritizes a special kind of lockdown protocol in the case of a missing or potentially abducted child. Still, it would be another two years, in 1996, before the nationwide AMBER Alert: America's Missing Broadcast Emergency Response, would radically change the way we respond to missing child's cases.

Topographically, 20 percent of Florida is wetland, while 45 percent is—*nope*, not pretty coastlines and lakes—dense forests. That means that Florida is a treasure trove of hiding places, leading the nation in most recovered unidentified bodies. Many of which were discovered in and around Yeehaw Junction.

CHAPTER SEVENTEEN

July 1, 1999. I sat in the shade outside Mr. Ollie's farm store funneling cat litter and nitrate into a grinder for sugar rockets. I lifted a tab on the baking soda and sprinkled it in, pushing down on a rusty ramrod to smooth the powder down to the blade. The base of the PVC pipe was hollow, crusty, ready for a light. Mr. Ollie, standing in the smoke by the grill, told me not to blow my brains out as he flipped hot dogs and sloppy joes.

"I don't got any brains," I said.

I blended the snow white nitrate crystals and pebbly cat litter with a big wooden spoon. The kickball that Cricket and Bam Bam played with sanded my face as it flew by like a tumbleweed. Men with raised voices jumped out of semi trucks to buy something at the store. They ignored me when they walked past. A guy in a Buc-ee's trucker hat stalled at the door, glancing at Lil Rascal swaddled in a milk crate in the shade. Lil Rascal hadn't been looking so good. It quit making noise and turned a deadly shade of pale. It was like I could almost see right through it.

"Is that a baby you got there?"

"Well, it's not a golden retriever," I snapped, deep-throating a ketchup-smeared hot-dog in a sucking-dick motion, just to get the dude something to be mad about.

I ate the hot dog, closed the PVC pipe. I took a lighter out of my shorts and held it against the black mole on my hand. I got the flame as close as I could get it to my skin without flinching. Other marks on me were turning black, too. The pink and red welts on my other hand had dried out from the flame, black around the edges. I'd burn them off before they could get to me.

I popped open an RC Cola, scarfing down another sloppy joe that Mr. Ollie dumped on a paper plate. Too hot for a t-shirt, so sunny that looking up burned my eyes. I couldn't even wear the rescue vest, which was stuffed into the back of my camo shorts like a bandana.

Jenna was gone. Ziggy was gone. Starr was gone. Olivia was gone. Trudy was gone. Macon was gone. Kidnapped Heather was gone. President Clinton was even getting impeached. When they came for me, who did I have to shoot to be free? I thumbed the Discman's play-pause button, starting the Marilyn Manson CD over. I slipped on the fuzzy black headphones. If I got up to kick the kickball or piss in the grass, I hid the Discman in Lil Rascal's milk crate. Nobody would think to look next to a baby for a Discman. It wouldn't get snatched.

"Play spades?" I said.

Mr. Ollie wiped his hands off on an oily rag. Bobby, his nephew, was inside watching the store. "No, sir. I got work."

It was almost the 4th of July, my second favorite holiday only to Father's Day because that's when Cricket made a day of it. The year before last, she climbed on the roof of Mr. Ollie's farm store and announced she wasn't coming down until her daddy's kerfuffle soul got saved. Cricket liked Father's Day. It reminded her that there was always the roof to jump off, if things got too hard. I let that whirl around in my brain for a long time, and I liked the feeling it gave me.

When I looked up from my sugar rockets, the man in black beckoned me. He was across the way standing on the steps to the Desert Inn upstairs bar where Trudy had once worked. I could feel his breath in my ear, hear him whisper, even though he wasn't standing anywhere near me.

Radium and lead in youngblood's head. Everything goes to hell.

"Hey!" I waved to Cricket and Bam Bam, who were playing with a kickball. "Cheese it, let's roll!"

Mr. Ollie agreed to watch Lil Rascal for twenty minutes and not a minute longer. Set his watch and everything. I collected the sugar rockets, grabbing a container of powdered sugar left over from last New Years. It was sprinkled with cockroach eggs, so I might need to mix it with the nitrate if the explosion didn't take. I didn't take my eyes off the man in black. His jowl quivered.

"Come on, hurry up," I said, and Cricket and Bam Bam joined me in the street.

The man in black came down the stairs, about forty paces ahead of the rest of us, leading the way.

He turned toward Chicken Hill and went through the open gate.

Of course, the man in black was gone by the time we got to Chicken Hill. Some chickens squawked nearby, acting foolish like chickens do when they're running around. We tramped through the junkyard. No sign of the man. No sign of anybody except the Packard cars and old farm trucks, the usual mess. There was a balled mound of yellow splat from the constant Florida pollen staining anything that was tied down. I heaved a tire out of the way, so I could make room for the fireworks. Cricket sneezed. It wasn't dark yet but just twilight enough to make it look like the stars were fizzing out of the sky down over us.

Cricket took out her safety poncho and draped it around her. Then she sat on the tire and put her fingers in her ears. Bam Bam, used to explosions and a little fire-starter himself, climbed on top of a smashed trailer. There was broken glass everywhere. The crusher pile near the old guard house was still flipped on its side; gravel, dirt, rusted lunch boxes, and a layer of grime over a mountain of trash. The light of day folded up over the piston crusher. I wasn't afraid of it anymore.

I laughed, tossing Bam Bam the wheel off a Dodge so he could pretend to steer after lighting the first rocket. Cricket hollered. She blew the survivor kazoo, then quickly put her fingers back in her ears.

And then my bomb blew up, no mercy. The crackling speared up across the vanishing day and into flames everywhere. The sound seemed to shake the ground. I laughed, cheering for Bam Bam. Cricket blew the survivor kazoo again. There was another blast, another flame, and a blast after that, all of my successful sugar rockets dumping ash back into the earth.

For a moment, my eardrum closed. I couldn't hear a thing. Bam Bam was talking but I couldn't hear it. My vision blurred but returned. One of the Packards on the mountain blew up when the rocket returned to earth and didn't ignite all the way until it hit steel, going faster than it had going up. Bam Bam jumped off the Chevy and joined me and Cricket by the tires, backing up instinctively at the blast, the glass raining over us. Half-peeled tires struck by the nitrate scorched the guard house and exploded midair.

Radium and lead in youngblood's head. Everything goes to hell.

My eardrum opened up. Bam Bam and Cricket coughed. Cricket asked if I was okay.

I waited for the smoke to settle. I walked to the mountain of trash, climbing up what was left of the Packard and tires, deadwood, and up the old horizontal guardhouse where Olivia and I once stood smoking cigarettes during the search. I sidled up to the guardhouse–the door was missing. A bureau with broken drawers half stuck out of the side. I couldn't move the bureau but I could move the drawers. I wedged them out of their holes and they rolled down until they hit the dirt ground below. I was covered in grit, smoke. Sweat dripped down my ass crack. I leaned forward to get a better look, as Cricket and Bam Bam climbed up the broken trailer behind me. There in the guardhouse, a young girl looked back at me.

CHAPTER EIGHTEEN

10 the Hour, Every Hour ... on MTV
August 27, 1999

The San Francisco Report called it "the day the music died." It's been one month since the barbaric atrocities of the Woodstock 1999 music festival in upstate New York. And this time, we can't blame Marilyn Manson.

Although cleanups continue at the former festival grounds outside of Syracuse, the emotional impact of the trauma for the concert attendees has a much longer rehabilitation road in front of it.

With 400,000 in attendance and temperatures reaching 101 degrees Fahrenheit, unruly looting, vandalism, substance abuse, and a perceived atmosphere of misogyny was only the beginning. One thing was certain: women were unwelcome in the crowd and the stage. The National Organization for Women have facilitated protest marches against the sexual violence that transpired during the festival. Eight rapes and two gang rapes were reported in the mosh pit during headliners' performances on festival days one and two. Three women were killed in the crowd and hundreds more had their clothing torn. Even female artists scheduled to perform were pelted with feces, water bottles, groped, and booed offstage. The crowd demanded in nonstop sweeping chants, "Show us your tits!"

The water stations set up for concert-goers to stay cool during the heatwave were contaminated with toxic levels of E. Coli after pipes broke. The American Red Cross treated over 5,000 people for dehydration and various injuries, which later led to a trenchmouth outbreak in the state of New York, just weeks ago.

Marilyn Manson, scheduled for the Saturday afternoon slot, allegedly dropped out of Woodstock at the last minute after a shaky few months undergoing scrutiny and criticism in the wake of the Columbine massacre in Colorado. It seems Marilyn Manson is the least of America's problems. Forty-five men were arrested after Woodstock and Marilyn Manson wasn't one of them.

Music festivals and concerts around the globe have been cancelled in light of Woodstock's atrocities. The U.S. Department of Health and Human Services is requiring venues, artists, and concert promoters to restore and enforce crowd-safe conditions and improved security before commencing live music events. 1999 has produced irrevocable changes to the live music industry and America's culture war with itself.

CHAPTER NINETEEN

JULY 3, 1999. It was the day everything went to hell. I knew exactly how it would go, too.

A whining siren on the roof of a piggie's cruiser would light up the whole street blue and red. I'd be hidden behind the Florida-room door, and I'd see the piggie's hunchbacked shadow lumbering up the porch stairs. One *bang* through the brain and he's fallen down on the wood, dead. And we'd go running and make it out alive before the other pigs could be upon us.

Lil Rascal used to fuss but now it was quiet all the time because the baby was dead. Mr. Ollie pointed it out to me, as if I didn't fucking know. I was keeping the little corpse around for Cricket, who couldn't really know the difference. Save face and all of that.

But for now, the house was quiet except for the occasional truck that zoomed by, or the dumb dog next door barking when it heard nothing. It smelled like cunt in here.

Me and Kidnapped Heather were sitting side by side on Trudy's old mattress. The aluminum foil over the windows was peeling in the corners, so the sun trickled in something harsh. Bam Bam helped me drag the T.V. into the bedroom from the living room, so I could watch MTV playing the '99 Woodstock commercial. I looked at Kidnapped Heather to make sure she was watching the parts with Marilyn Manson. She didn't talk much, I'd come to find. Some girls don't. Olivia never could shut the fuck up. Kidnapped Heather was different.

"Marilyn Manson's gonna be there," I said. I lit up a cigarette, a Newport, eager to share with her. I let go of the spark, and tossed the lighter at her, trying to get a reaction. "You deaf? I said Marilyn Manson's gonna be there."

Kidnapped Heather had gotten cleaned up real good since we found her in Mr. Ollie's junkyard. Cricket helped peel off her filthy clothes and gave her fresh underpants and Macon's WWJD? t-shirt. She even clipped some of Mallory's old hair to the top of Kidnapped Heather's head, for her to wear. It was nice of Cricket to part with some of it. Make the new girl feel a part of something.

"You like T.V.?" I said. "I like T.V., sex, violence, and then more T.V." I clicked my tongue. "Come on, you know we weren't the ones that kidnapped you? Look at me. I'm just trying to protect you."

Kidnapped Heather locked eyes with me. She always looked on the verge of cry-baby tears. There was a half-eaten dagwood on the bed. Not even on a paper plate, but hanging out there on the bed where it had fallen out of her hand because she got fatigued or some shit. Mustard and mayo everywhere.

"Trudy would have a cow if she saw we were eating dagwoods on her bed," I laughed. "Fuck Trudy."

I blew smoke into Kidnapped Heather's face. She returned her gaze to the T.V.

"What did you do that whole time? The whole time you were, you know, kidnapped. You don't remember who did it or nothing. But you had to do something to pass the time."

Kidnapped Heather blinked. She said, "I don't remember."

"Sure you do."

"I don't."

I took my lighter back, playing with the flame. If she was gonna play games, so was I. "You're one of us now; one of the youngbloods. The four of us, that's all we need. We're gonna fuck the feds, kill the pigs, blow up the schools, hit up New York, and meet Marilyn Manson. Look, the world's gone to hell out there. Don't believe me? Well, you were gone a long time. The year 2000 came and everything went to hell."

Kidnapped Heather narrowed her gaze. "What happened?"

"Shit hit the fan when the computers switched to 1/1/00. Bombs dropped. Armies raided homes. We're some of the last people that made it out alive. Why do you think nobody's coming looking for you here?" I exhaled smoke. "Marilyn Manson made it out."

"Thank you, Skeet," Kidnapped Heather said.

"No sweat. Smoke?"

She shook her head.

"I know your friend," I said. "Olivia. She was nasty to me. She came onto me, acted like a real bitch."

"I don't know Olivia," Kidnapped Heather said.

"Sure you do," I said. "I just don't know why she was such a snob. Why didn't she want to put a bullet in the gun? I didn't ask her to fire it. I don't care. I was going to invite her into the gang if she wanted to ditch school and her folks. But she's just a little kid, which makes you think."

"It does."

I put my arm gently around Kidnapped Heather. Her shoulders trembled. Her hands were balled into fists. "You're so beautiful," I said, raking thick strands of Mallory's old hair between my fingers. "Can I kiss you? I want to kiss you."

I leaned in, quickly giving her a pop on the forehead. Her forehead was dimpled with pimples and scratch marks. Guess she tried to get away once or twice.

"You're different. You're not like other girls."

Kidnapped Heather looked toward the doorway. She unballed her fists, looking down into her palms, then she looked at mine. "Why's there blood under your fingernails?"

I looked at the grit. "Maybe from helping you out of the hole."

Kidnapped Heather seemed satisfied with that answer. She showed me her splinters. I asked if she could see sunlight from the guardhouse. Or was it always dark? How did she breathe? How did she not suffocate in the dank humidity? What did she eat? What did she drink?

Cricket and Bam Bam came into the bedroom with stacks of dagwoods like in a cartoon strip. Bam Bam was wearing his Monica Lewinsky mask. Cricket's eyes were lit up when she saw Kidnapped Heather awake and alert on the mattress.

"I got a surprise for you," Cricket cooed. She pulled the survivor kazoo out of her jean shorts pocket and blew it. "Go ahead and try it. Blow it once, for practice. Twice, for luck. Three times, that's for joy."

Kidnapped Heather trembled as she took the survivor kazoo from Cricket. She started crying, too. Not weeping, but tears formed in her eyes, making them all red and splotchy again. She blew the kazoo and cried harder.

"That's it!" Cricket said.

Kidnapped Heather blew the survivor kazoo again. She stumbled out of bed, wobbling like a broken toy, poor balance and everything, then turned the corner by the dumpy air conditioning unit and fell. Bam Bam pushed back his Monica Lewinsky mask and helped her back on her feet.

"Where are you going?" Cricket asked. "You have to blow the kazoo again."

Kidnapped Heather blubbered, pointing toward the door.

"Don't make this harder than it needs to be," I said.

Cricket pulled Kidnapped Heather back toward Trudy's fuckpad mattress. The dagwood slid down against her bare legs. Bam Bam grabbed a pillow (no pillowcase) from the floor, nudging it behind her. Cricket said, "You're a survivor now. Me too. We can be survivor girls together. Do you know what that means?"

Kidnapped Heather looked at the T.V.

"It means, silly dilly," Cricket smiled. "You get a Survivor's Day, like me. You'll never be hurt again and they send you a cake in the mail every year."

We spent the evening dyeing our hair with what Trudy had around the bedroom. We used tubes of blue and black, looking just like a bruise. Cricket was careful not to dye Mallory's stolen hair–she wanted to keep that blond, pure. A memory of Mallory. Kidnapped Heather cried as Cricket and Bam Bam rubbed the smelly black chemical through her scalp. It got everywhere, especially on her neck. It seeped into the mattress.

Cricket had the time of her life doing Kidnapped Heather's hair, and after she blew it dry, she took out Trudy's old horse brush and asked if she could brush her hair.

"One, two, three," said Cricket, pulling long, even strokes.

Between tears, Heather begged us to find her mom.

Cricket nudged her. "Say it with me–one, two–your turn."

"Three," Heather chirped.

"No," Cricket said. "One, two, three, *brush*; one, two, three–"

"Brush."

"One, two, three–"

A snot bubble popped out of Kidnapped Heather's nose. "Brush."

"That's right, you got it," complimented Cricket.

Bam Bam had dressed Lil Rascal's corpse in some baggy baby overalls. He thought the baby looked funnier in the overalls dead than when he was alive and fussing all over the place.

Because I'd gotten more feral, more dangerous, I kept the Survivor's Day handgun on me and nothing else. So I was ready when the shadow man came to the door. For a split second, I thought it might be the man in black, but it was a piggie. I wasn't imagining things. I saw the lights in the street before I heard the wicked siren.

I told the others to be quiet, stay in the bedroom, and turn up the T.V. as loud as it would go. I crawled down the hallway to the kitchen and around the corner to the entry of the Florida-room. Then, I crouched beside the shopping cart where nobody could see me. The piggie announced himself, like they always do before they're slinging two paces too fast and wiping people out.

I pointed the gun at the piggie. My hands turned hot, gripping the thing. I pulled that trigger. It was my first time doing it. I thought I blew my ear off but it was just my eardrum humming out again. The sound of the *click* like a Discman skipping tracks.

The siren on the cruiser still rang. I kicked the dude in the face to see if he'd move, and he didn't, not a hair. His mustache was soaked in his own pulpy gray matter. A perfect circle in the center of his head. The dog next door barked batshit again.

We got a move on. We went on foot: me, Cricket clutching Lil Rascal for dear life, Bam Bam, and Kidnapped Heather; one behind the other, like scouts on a camping trip. We hiked and ran as long as our bodies would take us, past the electrical pylons, the tractors in the prairie, the sound of I-60 traffic in the distance. Out of habit, I looked back once over my shoulder for either Macon or Jenna and was relieved not to see them.

We heard more sirens coming for us about two miles from the Salida Preserve, somewhere north a ways. Bam Bam walked backwards because he saw it in a movie once, to cover his tracks in the wetlands. Only we weren't in the wetlands, we were in the scrubs and palmettos, and trying to keep as quiet as possible. Kidnapped Heather was good at that: keeping quiet.

"I miss Trudy," Cricket said, breathlessly. "Can we pick her up?"

"I don't want to hear nothin' about Trudy," I said. "She left us to the wolves. Fuck her."

"Woof," Bam Bam said.

The brambles tore at our clothes and scratched our skin. We had to keep picking up our knees to get through. It hurt the longer we hiked, and it got hotter the further the sun got away from us. I thought that was bad until the rain came out. The air was so moist, it had a little suffocation to it. Made you feel twice your weight. I let the mosquitos take me, the thorns, the brambles, the whole fucking land. I looked down and my ankles were dripping with blood. I thought about leaving Lil Rascal in the woods. It would've been easy to abandon a baby that didn't cry.

"We're in Florida," Kidnapped Heather remarked.

"We're going to New York," I said. "We're going to see Marilyn Manson at Woodstock '99."

Cricket beamed. I couldn't see her face but I could hear it in her voice. "New York's a nice place, Skeet. That's where the White House is and the Burdines store. They give you a passport if you visit New York. Lil Rascal's gonna be a world traveler someday."

Bam Bam removed his Monica Lewinsky mask at nightfall. We got to Withlacoochee State Forest, the farthest we'd ever hiked in our lives. Gnats were stuck to our faces and lovebugs fucked on the backs of our knees. The world was suddenly like a roach I was gonna crush under my shoe.

We moved cautiously and froze any time the sirens came. We'd stay stony-faced-still in the dirt until the lights were gone. I could hear helicopters. We wondered how long it would take to trek to the mining quarry. Jenna had once offered to bury Macon up in the quarry but Trudy said the drive would be too risky—although look who was behind bars. Not Jenna.

The river was murky and black, not shimmery under moonlight like the lake back home near Yeehaw Junction. Too many longleaf pines leaned over us. Mossy canopies weeded through brambles that dropped ten feet down into the quarry. We had to crawl down the limestone, so the helicopter lights wouldn't find us. We drank from the river on empty stomachs. Lil Rascal was so lifelessly limp in Cricket's arm, I forgot he wasn't a doll. The rain blew sideways and the palm fronds hit us on the head until we got to another clearing encircled by endless timber and longleaf pines. And then the knuckled ridge where the quarry would get us to the other side.

Kidnapped Heather thanked me for saving her from the bad guys as we came upon a hundred-year-old excavator, half sunken and eaten by the natural earth. She begged me not to let her go, let her get lost again.

But our journey through the quarry took all night because of Lil Rascal and the dense, moonless paths we stumbled down in the dark. It was hard to see. I checked for the Survivor's Day handgun all the time. I checked for the Jesse James cap gun, too. Extra protection. Only once did Kidnapped Heather attempt to leave the three of us. I held her close, though, swore to her she could blow the survivor's kazoo when we got to New York.

"If it's really the new millennium, Skeet," Kidnapped Heather said, wiping away her tears. "Then why are the police looking for us? How come there were so many cars on the road? How come–"

Bats clipped the sky. There was a sign about amoeba warnings where the river curved into limestone rocks again, and more broken machinery and cinder blocks blocked our path. We'd have to climb again. Bam Bam was starting to lose speed. My dogs were barking, too.

We drifted through the rain as it picked up, winging branches into our path. I put the fuzzy black headphones over my head, but it was getting harder to hold the Discman and the CD skipped.

The first sign we saw, other than the amoebas warning, was for Ocala.

Bam Bam stopped in his tracks, coughed something nasty into his hand, then threw up all over the ground. Kidnapped Heather suggested we stop and let everybody rest. I said whoever wanted to ditch out and not walk the rest of the way could fend for themselves out here until daylight, but I wouldn't be back. I was going to New York. I wasn't worried about Lil Rascal or hopping onto a train or stealing a car, or walking all the way there in my wet, broken chucks.

"It's hot out here," Bam Bam said. He'd lost the Monica Lewinsky mask somewhere in the quarry.

"Don't I know it," I said, nudging Kidnapped Heather. "Fix your face, girl. Don't cry. We're not gonna hurt you. We don't hurt anybody that don't deserve hurting."

"He's right," Cricket said. "Except my daddy."

"Except your daddy, Cricket," I said.

We hauled ass the rest of the way, gaining a second wind when daylight reared its head on the horizon.

CHAPTER TWENTY

Last Statement by Gertrude 'Trudy' McLeod
Filmed on July 3, 2025 for documentary film (*Untitled*, 2026)
LOWELL CORRECTIONAL INSTITUTION
OCALA, FLORIDA

I'm Samantha Micelli, a documentarian from Los Angeles. I've landed in bustling, sunny Orlando, Florida to drive north to attend the state execution of notorious foster mother and child abductor, Trudy McLeod. Trudy's now seventy-five years old with declining health. She relies on a walker and receives federally-funded breast cancer treatment.

Today—July 3, 2025, at seven o' clock—Trudy McLeod will meet her fate, after being denied an eleventh-hour appeal to the Governor of Florida. She is giving us, and the rest of the world, the opportunity to tell the unfiltered, integral truth about her involvement in the

June 14th, 1999 abduction of eleven-year-old Heather Studebaker, who is still missing today.

Trudy McLeod was originally arrested, not for her alleged involvement in the Heather Studebaker case, but for the unrelated, alleged abduction of a baby boy named Angel Stanton from Jacksonville General Hospital's pediatric ward in 1987. That baby boy, whom Trudy identifies as "Skeet," is also still missing.

After a lengthy and expensive investigation and trial, Trudy McLeod was convicted of five counts of first-degree murder, charges of premeditated kidnapping, obstruction of justice, child endangerment, and welfare fraud.

In 2003, Trudy was sentenced to death.

Trudy McLeod herself was a victim of childhood abduction. In 1955, in Broken Arrow, Oklahoma, a young girl walked by herself to the school bus stop. She was abducted by a couple: Donovan Ellis and Lindsay Ellis. She was kept in captivity for thirty days until officials located her at the couple's home near Oklahoma City. Her name was Amanda Lancaster then, a popular eleven-year-old girl from a broken home. After being rescued, Amanda was sent to a foster home in Ocala, Florida, where she lived with two foster siblings and step-parents. She acquired a new identity, that of Gertrude "Trudy" McLeod.

The case turned full circle in the summer of 1999, when similarities arose with the Studebaker abduction. For example, Heather was the same age as Trudy when she went missing on the back roads of Fort Drum, Florida.

Now, I'm sitting with McLeod in a bright, accessible sunroom usually occupied by women for socializing during their life without parole sentences.

The rest is her story.

§

My name is Trudy McLeod, Inmate 04102785-FCL.

The think tanks know me as Trudy, but call me Mandy. That's not a radical request when I've got less than twelve hours of life left, max. I accept the prayer of the Church of Latter-Day Saints, and thank them for their inclusion of a woman battered by the failed assistance systems in the U.S. of A. I'd like to thank the Florida Governor. I'd like to thank my county of conviction, Orange County. I'd like to thank the Lowell Correctional Institute because without them, I'm waiting to hurt somebody that's asking for it. I'm hoping that by disclosing what I know, without a defense attorney present, without the media, without the talking heads, that I'll be given a little more breathing time.

See that blue bug zapper in the corner ceiling, up there? Well, they keep that in here because of moths and hissing palmetto bugs that turn white as a sheet. The white ones gross me out. Ugliest crawlies you ever did see. Would you know that that neon blue zapper is the brightest light I see all day? Not the sunshine. Armchair detectives tell me I don't deserve sunshine anymore. Well, everybody's got an opinion just like everybody's got an asshole. *Me Too*, isn't that what women say these days? *Me Too*. They march in their pussy hats, disgraced that *Roe v. Wade* was overturned, as if that turn of events hadn't been hanging on by a thread when they elected the Bushes and their country horses years before Trump. Yes, I watch YouTube, I read the papers. I'm not brain dead just because I'm behind bars.

Pay attention. That's what I have to say to America, to anybody watching this. Pay attention.

I'm a southern woman without a lot of fucking rug under me. My therapist calls it survivor's defense, survivor's guilt, survivor's problems. Put that under your pussy hat. How much self-care do we need to solve the mystery of Heather Studebaker's disappearance? How blind do you gotta be to still not know who did it?

There's a lot of worms in Yeehaw Junction. A lot of cold blooded murder. A lot of magpies and fish to fry. When it's hot, it boils. Do you know what I mean when I say that—*when it's hot, it boils*? Your organs can cook when the temperature gets to a certain degree. What does that do to your brain? It cooks it.

Amoebas. There's brain-eating amoebas in our waters, lead, chloroform, and nitrates. Drink water out of the hose or out of the kitchen sink, let that water soak into your pores when you're bathing, and come back to me when you get pathology to confirm that your body is spiked with cancer. God, you should hear me coughing at night. Chemo don't work if you've been exposed to DDT. Chemo rejects it way before your body rejects the DDT.

I've got breast cancer: invasive small cell carcinoma, stage 3, mets. It hurts to cough, hurts to breathe, hurts to sleep. Don't worry, I'm not going to bounce out of this chair and strangle you like Hannibal Lecter or something. I can barely walk. I haven't been dangerous in a long, long time.

Let's see. I'm nervous. But I want to tell my story. I'm from Broken Arrow, Oklahoma, but I was practically raised in Ocala, here in Florida.

Did I abduct Heather Studebaker? No.

Did I kill Heather Studebaker? No.

Was the abduction premeditated and was I involved? Yes.

Let me give it to you straight. Abducting a human being, much less a child—that's up to here in height—is a tall order and I wasn't going to do it. That's her body. That's not mine. Take it from a survivor of sexual assault, childhood abduction—you name it, I've lived it. Take it from a survivor, period. Talk to us. We're all here, scraping by in this facility pen. Go to the cells, talk to the women.

I knew that if a little white girl went missing and the odds of ciphering what happened to her *looked* grim, *looked* like a stranger abduction, that nonprofits, moms, the FBI, everybody in the fucking world, would be offering money in exchange for either information or her body returned.

Yes, kids go missing every day but most of them are found alive within twenty-four hours. I was going to forge this from a smarter place. But you've got nothing on me now, other than my confession, which, by the time anybody even sees this, I'll either be right where I am on death row indulging in my free healthcare and three hot meals a day, or I'll be dead by lethal injection. Your organs cook during that, too.

My crime, my real crime, my honest-to-God belly buster, that I pled guilty to before a televised grand jury in the fall of 2003, was that I abducted a baby boy named Angel Stanton from a pediatric ward at Jacksonville General Hospital in 1987. Women like me, we're always five steps ahead of you. Believe that. Covering my tracks is something I'm good at.

In 1987, I was working custodial. I'd been there a couple years already. This was the decade everybody got rich except for me. I'd been fired from Jerry's Joint, a biker bar in Daytona. I moved. I spent ninety days in jail for possession of marijuana during a hit and run, and I got the custodial job.

Angel Stanton. I knew this baby boy's name wasn't Angel. There was no Angel in his eyes. God have mercy on me and on him. The minute I picked him up out of that miserable crib, I knew his name was Skeet. Skeet was actually an Alabama baby. He was in Florida getting treatment; for what, I don't know. It's not my business; like I said, that's his body, not mine. I premeditated his abduction, like Heather Studebaker's, for several months. I paid attention. I didn't know which baby I was going to take, or, if I was even going to go through with it. I knew the risks. I also knew about the mythical systems the American government perpetuates on its people that can't pay their medical bills, the medical bills they *caused* by making us sick, sending the poor to do dirty work, swimming in lakes full of poisons that they dumped there, you name it.

I knew the pediatric ward like the back of my hand. I cleaned bathrooms, emptied trash cans, dumped soiled linens into shoots; scrubbed this, that, and the other. Dealt with nurses that needed attitude adjustments. I was around for all of it. Pediatrics was the only floor that required a key card at the time. I had a key card and made rounds after I punched into the timeclock.

One of the correctional officers here in LWP told me they punch in to work now on their phones. Isn't that something? You see, we didn't have surveillance back then.

I'm not calling him Angel. His name is Skeet.

I took Skeet into the restroom with me and gently laid him inside of an empty receptacle bag. Lots of holes in the bag, of course. He wasn't in any danger of suffocating, although if he had been any older, he'd have probably thrashed around like a cat. I tied the receptacle bag to the electric floor scrubber, and I turned the electric floor scrubber on, so nobody could hear him screaming. An orderly would have had to physically open this receptacle to see the baby inside, but that was a risk I took and in retrospect, I had some big balls on me.

I pushed the electric floor scrubber out into the hallway, emptied the orderlies' paper waste bins. Scrubber's turned all the way. I heard commotion among the nurses across the hallway, and I just kept doing my job, kept pushing that machine. Police arrive, I'm still cleaning. I get in the elevator, return the scrubber to maintenance. I was alone. It was the graveyard shift. I took the receptacle to my car and Skeet was mine, as far as I was concerned. I returned to the building while the baby was on the floor of my car, and I punched my timecard. Done and done.

Staff called for a Code Pink. They say Code Adam now, but back then it was Code Pink. Everybody was carrying on about a missing child upstairs. Well, the next day the police interviewed me. They interviewed everybody that worked that day and they reviewed security footage from the south unit. Didn't have a damn thing on me. No more than the cafeteria lady or the gut surgeon or a custodian taking extra long smoke breaks on the floor below me.

How could anybody harm a baby? I couldn't. I didn't. I couldn't harm nobody if they weren't asking for it. But people do it. And I'm surrounded by women in here that've hurt people, even their own children.

My other crime, the other Big Dipper crime, the reason I'm on death row waiting my turn for lethal injection, is because I killed my oldest foster child, Macon Delaney. I was convicted on three counts of first-degree murder for Macon. I pled guilty. It was televised, case closed. Again, not why I was first arrested, but the truth comes out. Always does. God makes it so.

Macon's last words to me were, "Help me, Mama. Please."

I was never his mama. Oh, and you can carve "Hard Ass" on my hip at the execution table, if you want to. But I was never his mama. I was his guardian. I killed Macon in cold blood. I lost my temper learning what the kids did off the turnpike, causing a goddamn ten vehicle pile-up. Two deaths, four injuries, *good God*, I was enraged and I knew Macon was the knucklehead behind it. I'd planned to take off with the kids the next day, just fucking go. But Yeehaw Junction had other plans.

How did I kill Macon? I held his head under the pool water for thirty minutes. It took that long. Yes. I spent thirty minutes trying to stop his breathing. It takes longer than you think. See, I'm a nocturnal worrier. Something went off inside of me and I didn't want him around me anymore. I held his neck like this, gripped in my arm, sort of held his body at a bizarre angle for a few minutes. He tried fighting me, of course, but I had the upper hand because I wasn't the one with what was probably a concussion, zonked out in the pool. Thirty minutes. It took that long. I was exhausted by the end of it.

Macon was about to turn eighteen. He was either gonna make some woman miserable or kill himself, get himself arrested. My $450 was about to get cut once he turned eighteen. I got Macon when he was about eight years old. A friend let me have him. She had too many babies, and he was the hardest of the pack. I didn't want him trafficked to some sick sex ring, so I took him in.

It's a funny system, it is. I got more money from fostering that boy than his mama got from the government when she was working full-time and trying to take care of him. That's the funny part of being a woman, too. If I'd been working custodial, on my own volition had a baby, I'd get called irresponsible. Maybe even foolish or selfish. Making ends meet, that's what it's about, right? But if I'd already had the baby—Skeet, in this instance—and I was scrubbing shit off public toilet lids, well, in that case I'm just a bread-winner. I'm just providing. I'm a *mom*.

Look at things with a different lens and it's the same.

Okay. I'm up-to-date.

I've got more confessions in me.

Me and Skeet were both victims of abduction. We had that connection. We'll have that connection forever and ever. Nobody can take that away from us. I don't know where Skeet is today, and, yes, I do think about him. He'd be thirty-eight years old now, wouldn't he? Do I think he actually made it out alive past the year 1999? No. Absolutely not. That boy was dumber than a box of rocks. He had a violent streak in him. He was going to be my violent boy, he was.

Yes, I orchestrated the abduction of Heather Studebaker.

I told Ziggy Calhout and Ollie Billings that I did not want this girl harmed. I didn't want her raped, beaten, not even underfed. I just wanted her locked away from the world for a while; don't let her see you, don't let her hear your voice, don't let her smell you.

We started planning this ordeal in 1998, agreeing that Ollie Billings–the kids called him Mr. Ollie–would hide her in the mining quarry at Withlacoochee State Forest out near Brooksville. That's less than a hundred miles from Yeehaw Junction; far, but not so far away that we were crossing state lines. There's nitrate there, too, uranium, in the quarry, heaven knows. Hasn't been in operation since 1901, so the only people that hike through the quarry are tech students from out-of-state that think they're pulling one over on southerners; and rotten people like myself, like Mr. Ollie, you get the picture. It's almost inaccessible. I'll give you a map of the park and you won't be able to locate it. I took the kids there in 1998. Even Bam Bam, my youngest, my biological son. I took the kids there. I told them I'd need them for a job next summer, but I didn't detail what that meant.

Well, snatching Heather was the hard part. I'm a firm believer that the closer you are to the danger, the safer you are from harm and the less traces you'll leave behind. Busy places with patrons and traffic and kids, that's the ideal place. Not like when I was kidnapped, on a lonely street after school. Neighborhoods are not ideal places. Believe me. I mean, look. Twenty-five years later and there's never been enough evidence to convict me of an accessory to her abduction. Armchair detectives can rattle off a hundred reasons why it was me, but show me the evidence.

Heather Studebaker's mother Dolores was one of our dirty rotten clients, one of Ziggy Coulhart's clients, specifically. He'd known Dolores for a couple years now. Ziggy, he was about twenty or twenty-one at the time. He was a mechanic at his uncle's auto shop in Kissimmee. Astral Engines, it was called. You know where I'm going with this. Ziggy had worked on Dolores' country-style van more than once. He'd watched this girl Heather tag along with her mama at Astral Engines. Well, in September of 1998, almost a year before we even went through with it, I get there to give Ziggy a ride after work. I see him with Dolores in the front window and the kid's hanging off of her. I knew that girl was going to be America's next pre-teen true crime obsession.

I paid attention. That's all it takes. It takes time and attention.

Well, Ziggy informs me that Dolores is one of his clients. Not just her car, but she semi frequently buys snuff films from Ziggy at the shop. In fact, she bought the same tape twice. I don't know why, I couldn't tell you that. It was a video of me, pouring an old man's ashes all over my tits, sprinkling it into my crotch, my *pussy*, if you will, and just playing for the camera. Dirty rotten is a voyeur type of industry. But people want to get off, and Dolores—no shame in that—she wanted to get off. She found a way to do it privately with the young dude not judging her at the mechanic.

That exchange began almost a year of grooming and waiting for the right opportunity, between Dolores, Ziggy, and Heather. Small talk. Ziggy finally disclosed to me and Starr and Mr. Ollie that he was almost positive that Dolores took Heather to that rest stop on Fridays for a donut before school. It was routine. Dolores told him this and there was about a week's worth of practice runs. We were running low on time because summer vacation would start at the end of June.

Ollie and Ziggy snatched Heather at the Fort Drum Service Plaza. Starr Babcock drove the Pontiac Firebird. Ziggy would be the grabber, Ollie would chloroform her just enough to disorient her, knock her out for a few hours. Starr would drive.

Here's where we fucked up. Starr was supposed to drive to Withlacoochee Forest. Well, unfortunately, Starr couldn't commit to a coffee order, much less a proper kidnapping. She panicked, hit that gas, and went tearing off the exit ramp south instead of north.

You can imagine my rage when they showed up to Yeehaw Junction with that girl.

I was at work. I worked upstairs in Stickey's titty bar, mostly bartending. Ollie came to get me. The kids were off selling their jars for scraps—it gave them something to do, kept them out of my hair until nightfall. Anyway, I was the only one with a key to the back pantry at Stickey's. Not the refrigerators, but just the pantry where we kept things like napkins, peanuts. We didn't even wait until after hours to move Heather. The bar patrons were already distracted, drinking, tired of truck driving on the road, drunk. It wasn't difficult to sneak this comatose kid up the stairs between us and into the back rooms. I had the key. We kept her there for a few days. Me and Starr spent after hours bleaching everything so nothing could be traced, not even a hair from her little head.

When her disappearance got reported, I wanted to get her to the quarry, but it was too risky, driving her all that way. I needed to locate this girl, turn her in, call it a day. But it was too soon, it was much too soon. The reward money wasn't even at $100,000 when we decided to move her body, and then the kids did some God-forbidden pranks on the interstate. Suddenly, I had worse problems.

That's when I called it: *Ollie-Ollie-Oxen-Free*. I was done.

I wanted out of the dark web business, or, what we called it, the dirty rotten market. I'd gotten too deep in. It was psychologically taking a toll on me. I was starting to feel unsafe around Ziggy. I was starting to feel unsafe about the men and women that he was supplying these video tapes and photographs to. How many suicide victims' panties can you sniff while rubbing one out for $500? It gets to you. I didn't want a handgun to protect myself. I don't like violence. Ask anyone—even my caseworker. Slow places like Yeehaw Junction thrive with slow women like me, believe it. It's true. The money I made went to rent, cigarettes, Ollie, Starr's lingerie that I preferred her to wear. There was a credit union that Starr had access to. It was in my old name, "Amanda Lancaster." It was supposed to be our getaway money, because everybody that's poor needs a getaway, a fast one, because something's gonna bite you in the ass and you gotta go.

We kept Jenna McLeod, my second oldest, relatively in the dark about what this abduction was really about. But she caught on. She wanted control of it, of Heather, the situation. I don't know what the hell she was planning. I couldn't tell you. You'd have to find Jenna and ask her. The town ain't but two miles long; how many places can you hide a little girl without getting caught?

I'm guilty of all of the above. I'm guilty of being the white trash that the judge at my sentencing said, "May God have mercy on your soul." I'm the *told-you-so* that women dislike so much. Let me ask you something. Have you ever heard of Yeehaw Junction before this? No. Then you've never heard of Sugar Bends, either. It's not on most maps. The buzzards come and that's all you are.

Oh—hear that? Phone's ringing. That's for me, it's the governor.

CHAPTER TWENTY-ONE

JULY 4, 1999. The funny thing about endings is, you don't know it's an ending until you're dead: reclaimed by nature, sticking a fork in it, pushing daisies. Even if you've got it coming, you won't know it until it's too late. That's what I thought when Cricket, Lil Rascal, Bam Bam, and Kidnapped Heather saw the man in black in front of the guava stand on the Fourth of July. Maybe we were dead and on our way to Hell.

The man in black drove an old Chevy. When he picked us up, I saw there was a *Have You Seen Me?* flier on his dashboard. He was the man from my visions, frowning, all in black, lacking color in his eyes, like when he beckoned me on the street and grabbed my hand in the murky water.

The engine ticked while the truck was idle. The sun materialized over the rim of the world. The others squashed in the back seat. I sat up front with the man.

"Where you headed?"

"Uh, New York," I said. "You a pig with a badge? You been watching me?"

The man in black glanced at me, then checked his rear view. "I can't say that I have. I'm not a cop. Happy Independence Day. Name's Aberdeen."

"Skeet."

"To New York, huh?"

"Yep, New York." I mentioned I was broke and that we'd want to steal from a Texaco unless he had a better idea. We were famished. Hadn't eaten in over seventy miles on foot and still had ways to go.

"What's in New York?" the man in black asked.

"Our friend, Marilyn Manson. We're going to Woodstock."

The man in black nodded. "What's that?"

"You wouldn't get it."

I slipped on my fuzzy black headphones. The CD quit working back in the quarry. I plucked it from the Discman, cleaned it with my spit, but it was damp in the grooves and the CD was scratched. I watched the birds land on the telephone poles, and naughty children lighting up sugar rockets in the street. The wrenching vista of tamarind trees, live oaks, cows and chickens. A firework went off in the distance. Even in the morning light, somebody liked to play with fire. I listened to the man in black's jaw click as it trembled.

"Why's your face doing all that?" I said.

"Lived in an area with insecticides back in the 1950s, southern Florida. They call that DDT. You don't hear about it anymore. Neurological damage, is all. Nothing that the sun can't shine on more today."

"I don't believe you," I said. "You're full of shit."

The man in black didn't take his gaze off the road. "You got it, too. Well, a version of it. They used to give you a health card back in my day. Those moles and welts on your hands—I had those as a boy. Guess we have something in common. Hey, you dropped something." He tinkered in his glove compartment and pulled out my Jesse James cap gun.

"Thanks," I said. "I use it for target practice. So, you really gonna take us to New York?"

"As God is my witness, my word is good."

But I was exhausted and fell into a dreamless slumber where I didn't see nothing for hours until Cricket reached through the passenger window and shook me awake. I was alone in the car. I gasped. Where was the man in black?

"Where did he go?" I said.

Everybody was surrounding the Chevy. Cricket, still grabbing my shoulder through the window; Bam Bam, holding Lil Rascal; and Kidnapped Heather, looking haggard but nervous, like she was trying to figure out what to do. I jumped out, wiped my eyes of sleep gunk.

"Where did the guy go?" I repeated.

"*Ollie-Ollie-Oxen-Free,* he's kidnapping me. Silly, we all fell asleep," Cricket smiled. "Like Dorothy and the Tin Man and Scarecrow and the Cowardly Lion when they fall over in the poppies before they get to Oz. But we're awake now, see? Look, Skeet, it's a sugarcane mill."

Smoke rose in the distance out of the sugarcane fronds. It stunk and was terribly humid. No trees, nothing.

"Where are we?" I said.

"This isn't New York," Kidnapped Heather said.

"Yeah, no shit," I said.

There was a sign leafed in crabgrass on the shoulder of the road up ahead. I asked Cricket what it said.

SUGAR BENDS

POP: 11,200

The four of us looked at each other like we were sharing one stupid brain cell. I couldn't take this shit anymore. I wasn't about

158

to take it from Trudy, couldn't wait on Trudy, and now Trudy, that bitch, was gone. Macon, Jenna, fuckhead Billy, Mr. Ollie, Starr, Olivia, Mr. Dukakis and his erection, those college kids smoking dope in the van. All gone. Doomed heat.

I spit on the ground, my lip and neck dripping with sweat, and told the three of them who was in charge. Me. I was. I was in charge and nobody could give me no lip. Kidnapped Heather started crying and I asked Cricket for the gun, which she handed over like she was prompted for a handshake.

"Can I hold it after you?" Cricket asked. "Mr. Ollie said. And we don't know how to drive, Skeet. We could get in big trouble." Her hair was knotted and damp, Mallory's old strands bobbied by a butterfly clip.

"No lip," I said. I looked everywhere for the man in black, for Aberdeen. But he was nowhere. He'd left us here in Hell.

Our shoes ground into the gravel as we started out again.

Then, two piggy cruisers came flying fast down the road. Here was our death sentence. One of the piggies oinked into a megaphone to stay where we were and put our hands behind our backs. Their cruisers stopped.

"Uh-oh!" Cricket said.

The piggies called for backup and one of them emerged from the driver's door, taking off his service cap like brains might grow there. He grabbed Bam Bam by the arm and pulled him, along with Lil Rascal's body, toward the cruiser. The rest of us instinctively backed up. The piggie oinked about us joining him at the police station.

The way they looked at Cricket—like *she* was in charge, like she was her daddy in the slammer, I didn't like that. I didn't like that they didn't know her the way I knew her. They didn't know who was really the leader, the mastermind who saved Heather and was going to kill the whole world with Marilyn Manson.

My cheeks got hot. I went lightheaded like I'd drank an entire bottle of Nyquil, my vision swimming. The anger was frantic, deafening, out of control as I felt the heat boil the inside of my body, my temper rising like the sugarcane smoke. I wanted a blast from the handgun and the bullet left that barrel, fuzzing warm in my hand, and went exactly where I wanted it to.

Cricket.

I got her in the middle of her back.

She didn't know the difference, not at first. That's how Cricket was. She was busy trying to follow the orders of the costumed piggies. She never could figure out that we hated the cops. That's why shooting her was better.

I tasted bile as I watched Cricket's body slam into the gravel. Grit flew up as her hair fanned around her. Her eyes bulged, one twice as wide as the other, and blood dripped out of her mouth. She looked like the electric clown out front of the Kmart that blew a fuse after too many quarters. I never saw her look so unnatural. I guess some people just aren't built to handle violence.

"Skeet!" Cricket cried. "You fibbed! You said you would never leave me!"

There was raucous shouting, glass breaking. My hands didn't shake this time. I smiled. Kidnapped Heather ran into the rows of sugarcane. Bam Bam was making a fuss as the piggies stuffed him into the back cruiser. The piggie doing it oinked something into his walkie-talkie as he lifted Lil Rascal out of Bam Bam's arms.

My welts burned lightning heat. I saw double as blood surged out of the back of Cricket's body. I left her and didn't tell her goodbye. I got in the Chevy and heard more cruisers in the distance. I could barely reach the pedals. Cricket begged me to stay and help her. (*You fibbed!*) I could hear her wailing all the way down the road, though I was going as fast as the gas would allow. If I hadn't spun away and made my escape, I might fly and let the amoebas get me.

It was better this way for me and Cricket both, because nobody knew her the way I knew her. She wouldn't be safe and happy as a clam if anybody else got ahold of her spirit. I thought about what Trudy used to say. That the closer you are to the danger, the better chance you've got of getting away. We were headcases, youngbloods. Everything was going to be alright now, even if the decay was perpetual.

Like I said, headcase. It's all how you look at it. You call chunks of water puddles. It's like when people quip, "What's the difference between a redneck and a hillbilly?"

The riddle changes but the answer is always the same.

White trash.

I'd never seen the ocean before. Maybe I could stop and see it before I drove to New York to blow up Woodstock with Marilyn Manson. I fished Cricket's survivor kazoo out of my pocket and blew into it the entire way.

STILL MISSING

Heather Elizabeth Studebaker
$10,000 REWARD

The FBI is offering a reward of up to $10,000 for information leading to the location of Heather Studebaker.

LAST SEEN: July 4, 1999

LAST KNOWN LOCATION: Sugar Bends, Florida, Bends County

DATE OF BIRTH: 04/04/1988

CURRENT AGE: 37

SEX: Female

RACE: White

EYES: Brown

HAIR: Dark Blond (at time of disappearance)

IF YOU HAVE ANY INFORMATION
PLEASE CONTACT: HOPE4HEATHER
555 - 407 - 5525

WANTED BY THE FBI

ANGEL 'SKEET' STANTON

ALIAS: Skeet Hooper

BIRTHDATE: January 9, 1987

LAST RESIDENCE: Yeehaw Junction, Florida

CURRENT AGE: 38

LAST SEEN: Van Buren, Arkansas

WANTED on approx: Murder (17 counts), Unlawful Possession of Firearms, Unlawful Flight to Avoid Prosecution, Arson of an Occupied Structure(s), Aggravated Kidnapping, Child Endangerment and Abduction, Grand Theft Auto

REMARKS: Heterochromia eyes, black moles on skull, forehead, torso, upper back, hands, both arms. If found alive, Angel Stanton should be considered armed and extremely dangerous. The FBI is offering a reward up to $25,000 for information leading directly to the arrest of Angel 'Skeet' Stanton. If you have any information concerning this person, please contact your local FBI office or the nearest American Embassy or Consulate.

FIELD OFFICE: Orlando, FL

oBITUARIES

Gertrude Amanda McLeod
October 1, 1949 - July 4, 2025
WF, born 10/01/49, was sentenced from Marion County on 10/07/03 for the 01/11/1987 abduction of a baby boy. She has been implicated in the deaths of several persons, including minors. She was executed on 07/04/2025 at Florida State Prison in Raiford, Florida.

"Jane Doe"
WF, born in approximately 1956, died by a single gunshot wound to the spine on 07/04/1999 near Sugar Bends, Florida.

"Baby Jane Doe"
WF, partially decomposed, deceased infant. Appearance premature. Born approximately June 1999 in Osceola County, Florida. Died on or around 07/04/1999, Florida. Parents both deceased.

ABOUT THE AUTHOR

Kayli Scholz (she/her) is a horror author living and writing in the wilds of Florida. She's the author of novels *Saint Grit* and *Black Rain Season*. Her short stories have appeared in several anthologies, including *Punk Goes Horror* and *Nightmare Diaries*. Her short stories have appeared in magazines and literary zines such as *Smitten Land, Dark Moon Digest, A Formal Invitation, Storychord, Atticus Review, The Fem*, and others. Scholz's short story in *WhiskeyPaper* was a semifinalist for Best Small Fictions 2016. She's currently working on a fourth novel and a collection of short stories.

ACKNOWLEDGMENTS

I'd like to thank FZ Boda and everybody at Moonstruck Books for their intrepid trust and dedication to their authors. Special thanks to Hnwinanda for designing the book cover. Thank you readers and friends: C. R. Foster, Shanae Morris, Emma Broadbent, Chloe, Natacha Porter, Lev Zlata, Don Smith, Buster, Frankie, Ash. Most of all, big love and thank you's to my partner, Serdar, for everything, always, forever.